The Witches of Dredmoore Hollow

by
Riford McKenzie

with illustrations by
Peter Ferguson

For Ethan and Brynn

Marshall Cavendish Corporation
99 White Plains Road
Tarrytown, NY 10591
www.marshallcavendish.us/kids

Library of Congress Cataloging-in-Publication Data
McKenzie, Riford.
The witches of Dredmoore Hollow / by Riford McKenzie. – 1st ed.
p. cm.
Summary: Strange things begin happening at Elijah's New England home just before his twelfth birthday in 1927, especially after two aunts he had never met whisk him away to Moaning Marsh, where he realizes that they are witches who need something from him in order to remove a curse.
ISBN 978-0-7614-5458-8
[1. Witches–Fiction. 2. Blessing and cursing–Fiction. 3. Aunts–Fiction. 4. New England–History–20th century–Fiction.] I. Title.
PZ7.M198633Wit 2008
[Fic]–dc22
2007029781

Book design by Vera Soki
Editor: Robin Benjamin
Printed in China
First edition
10 9 8 7 6 5 4 3 2 1

mc Marshall Cavendish
Children

The Witches of Dredmoore Hollow

Some Things You Choose.
Some Things Choose You.
–Phineas Dredmoore, 1724–1824

Contents

Part 1

Carnivorous plants employ savage snap-traps, sticky tendrils, and other botanical weaponry to ensnare and devour live victims, including insects, birds, and small animals. More than six hundred species have been documented; the most rapacious of these is *Nepenthes raja*, exclusive to the mountains of Borneo, which is known to consume small mammals, frogs, and lizards. Despite fanciful reports to the contrary, carnivorous plants do not attack human beings.

—Hodgeworth's Encyclopedia of Natural Science

1

One Hundred Signs of Trouble

THERE WAS A FEARSOME STORM BREWING OVER
Dredmoore Hollow. All day long I'd been jumpy and belly-
sick. The air was damp and heavy at dinnertime, and by
dusk a wall of purple clouds rolled in over Clabberclaw
Mountain. Those thunderheads twisted and turned like ghostly
snakes, a dark sign if I ever saw one. My trouble-bug, Jonah,
lay on the floor of his tin house, belly up, overcome with the
fits. Every last one of his prickly little legs twitched at the air
in warning. I sorely wished Grandma Ester was on hand to
interpret. No matter. As omens go, a hundred twitching legs
was about as bad as it could get.

I pulled on my boots and ran for the barnyard, hoping
to get the last of my chores done while there was still a
smatter of light in the sky. I called in our two cows, Dandy
and Bloomers, drained the icebox pan, cleaned the leaves
out of the cistern, split some kindling for the kitchen cookstove, and rounded up all the gardening tools and heaved

them into the barn. I finished it all in record time and ran back to the house just as the rain broke loose.

I kicked off my boots, raced up to my bedroom, and got under the covers, still wearing my knickerbockers and shirt. I left the hurricane lantern burning full blast on the bed stand. Even with the quilt pulled up over my head, I could hear Jonah tossing and twitching inside his little tin house. It would be a sleepless night for the both of us, no question about it.

It was a curse being so chicken of everything, but I couldn't help it. Most kids got over the spooks as they got older. Not me. It seemed like I was turning more lily-livered every day. It probably didn't help that I lived on a rickety farm out in the middle of nowhere. Our place was so far away from Cold Creek Junction that we didn't even have electricity yet, never mind that it was 1927 and the rest of New England was living high in modern times.

Our old farm had been in Mama's family on the Dredmoore side practically since the Pilgrims. Plenty of folks said it was haunted, and you wouldn't hear me call them liars. Sometimes at night, I heard voices up in the attic. Every now and then, I saw flickering lights over the Dredmoore family graveyard. One time I even saw a pair of spectacles float across the backyard and into the privy of their own doing. At least, I thought I did.

Of course, whenever I'd say anything, Poppers would just tell me I was letting my imagination get the better of me. He didn't go in for haunts and the like. Mama never said much either way, but I could tell she was on my side. My father was only five-foot-three and scrawny as a cornstalk, but he was too fixed on common sense to be afraid of anything. I inherited his stature, but not his disposition.

Now the wind started in. The big oak outside my window scratched against the house. The shutters shook, and the weather vane whistled like a runaway train.

Just then, the barn door set to banging. I cursed myself for being so sloppy. I'd left it open when I brought the cows in, and now the wind was trying to rip it off the hinges. That meant somebody would have to go out there and shut it.

In the dark.

In the storm.

That somebody would be *me*. I buried myself under the sheets and waited for the holler.

"Hey, Elijah!" Poppers was right on cue. "Think you could run out there and shut that barn door?"

I waited a long time, hoping he'd think I was asleep.

"Oh, yeah," he said. "I'd appreciate it if you'd put away the wheelbarrow while you're out there, too."

I pretended to snore.

"Longer you wait, the more chores I can think up."

He had no pity on me at all. He figured the only way to get me over my skittish inclinations was to make me do the scariest things he could think of.

"I'm going, I'm going!" I hollered back.

I knew better than to tell him about Jonah's leg twitching.

He'd threatened more than once to feed my trouble-bug to
the rooster. And I bet he would've done it, too, except he'd
have both Mama and Grandma Ester to reckon with. He
blamed Grandma for filling my head with superstitious
twaddle. Maybe he was right, but I would've given anything
to be as bullheaded and plucky as her. She even had her
own hot-air balloon that she took up every Fourth of July.

I grabbed two hurricane lanterns—one off my bed stand,
plus another for backup. I pulled the slingshot out from
under my pillow, put on my barn boots and my rain slicker,
and pounded down the stairs.

Outside, the air was damp and smelled of sulfur. I'd read in
the *Farmer's Almanac* that you don't ever want to be outdoors when it smells of sulfur because you're bound to get
struck by lightning. There was one fellow who got zapped
so hard that all they ever found was his mucking boots. I
considered going in and telling Poppers about that. But
I knew better. He'd just send me back out with an extra
helping of chores.

I kept tight to the house and watched the sky for thunderbolts. With each flash, I searched the barnyard, hoping to
make out the whereabouts of the wheelbarrow before I ran.

Away across the orchard, I saw the Plinketts' upstairs
lights go out, leaving the valley dark as chimney soot. The
wind was gushing in every direction. The gusts knocked me
around like a gunnysack, trying like the devil to blow out my
lanterns. There was nothing else to do but get it over with. I

stuffed the cuffs of my union suit into my boots to keep the spiders out, then I shot across the yard toward the barn.

A flash of lightning lit up the cupola on the roof and turned the weather vane a fiery gold. My boots made sucking noises against my bare feet. I tripped over the cultivator and sprawled chin-down in the mud. I cursed at the confounded plow and got back to my feet. Nobody in all of New England except my father still used a horse-drawn plow. He said he didn't trust anything with a motor. Mama said he was born in the wrong century.

I stumbled my way around the barnyard as fast as I dared till I thumped into the wheelbarrow. I shoved it into the barn, latched up the door, and was just about to hightail it back to the house when a sound caught my ear. The wind was whipping and howling so bad that I couldn't be sure, but I thought I could make out the growl of a motor.

I stepped out onto the road to get a look down toward Plinketts' farm, and at just that moment, two beams of light came streaming up the hillside, flashing me square in the eyes. I sprang toward the barn in such a blind hurry that I tripped over the cow trough. Both my lanterns fell into the water and went out with a *hiss*.

I was still flat out on the ground when a truck rolled up next to the barn and turned off its lights. I peered out from behind the cow trough. Who in the world was coming out to our farm on a godforsaken night like this? The only person in all of Dredmoore Hollow who owned an automobile was Mr. Plinkett, and his Ford truck was parked out in the middle of the field with a full load of fence rails.

A burly man got out of the truck. The fellow was built like a tree stump—short and sawed off, but as big around as a rain barrel. I couldn't make out his face, not even when the lightning flashed, because he wore a black coat with the hood pulled up.

He went around to the back of the truck and drug a wheelbarrow down off the bed. He threw in a spade, a burlap sack, and a dim-glowing lantern. Then he stepped away from the truck and let out a low whistle.

Something huge and hairy jumped down from the truck. It looked like a wolf, but about three times too big. Its shoulders rose up in a great hump of scraggly fur. It circled the truck with its nose to the ground, sniffing like a hound dog.

The hooded man held the lantern up and felt around in his coat pocket. He pulled out a gnarly twig and stuck it in his mouth. Then he stood there a while, just chewing on the twig and studying the barnyard.

Suddenly, his gaze turned in my direction . . . and stopped.

I held my breath and swallowed hard.

Was he looking at *me*? The opening of his hood was squared off right at me, but his eyes were lost in shadow.

The hunchback wolf lifted his muzzle from the ground, and his ears stood up. He went dead still. His nose pointed straight at me.

"C'mon, Jack!" called the man.

He grabbed hold of the wheelbarrow, and the pair of them started toward me.

2

Burrowing Ravenweed

I HAD READ IN *HODGEWORTH'S ENCYCLOPEDIA* that timber wolves are carnivorous predators. They will hunt down any weak or sickly animal within sniffing range. As I ran stumbling across the barnyard, it occurred to me that I looked about as weak and sickly as anything a wolf could hope for.

I stole a look back over my shoulder and saw the hooded man's lantern bobbing along in his wheelbarrow. The wolf was still at his side. They didn't seem to be in any particular hurry. Maybe they hadn't actually spotted me yet on account of the storm and the darkness.

It struck me just then that in my fit to get away, I'd headed up the old wagon road toward the Dredmoore family graveyard–the worst direction I could've gone. Blackberry briars grew thick as walls on both sides of the track, leaving me no place to go except straight toward the cemetery.

I made it a habit to stay well clear of that place. I was pretty sure it was haunted. I'd seen shimmering lights and heard unholy howling sounds. Poppers always snorted and told me I ought to quit reading nonsense storybooks. But I knew what I saw. And so did Mama. One time a pair of monstrous ravens moved into the graveyard. They were evil-looking things. They perched on the statue of Phineas Dredmoore and cackled at the top of their lungs for a whole week, till Mama and Grandma Ester finally drove them off.

I stumbled up to the iron gate, shaking and puffing, and stood there a long while with no idea what to do. Everything about that graveyard said KEEP OUT! Tombstones and statues poked up from the witchgrass, leaning every which way like crooked teeth. They lit up blue and eerie in the sparks of lightning. I could read the words on a few that were close to the gate:

Here lies
Andricus Dredmoore
1788–1849
To darkness wedded
In power dreaded
By lightning beheaded

◡

Gertrude Thistlemar Dredmoore
1802–1811
Dearest Daughter
O cursed be that moonless night
When thou commenc'd thy fatal flight

The Witches of Dredmoore Hollow

༄

RIP

**Prudence, Hope,
& Charity Dredmoore**

1780-1793

*Thrice blessed by thy births
Thrice robbed by thy deaths*

A howl rose from just a short ways down the wagon road, knocking me back to my senses. I spun around and saw the glow of the lantern bobbing toward me across the briar-tops. The hunchback wolf sniffed and snarled like he was hot on a scent and hungry for blood.

All of a sudden the graveyard didn't seem so spooky.

I shoved the gate open and scurried inside, shaking so badly I could barely think straight. There was no place to hide, just half-toppled tombstones all around me.

The sounds of the wolf and the wheelbarrow grew closer and closer.

There was a half-rotted oak tree up against the iron fence. It was my only hope. I scrambled up the tree and hid myself in a tangle of dead leaves and twigs, breathless and numb.

I'd hardly got settled into place when the man and the wolf stomped up to the iron gate. The man stood at the entrance and studied the graveyard. He was faceless on account of the hood, and he cast a fearful shape in the flashing lightning. I held my breath. *Was he searching for me?*

Finally, his glance fell on the tall statue in the middle of the graveyard–the stone image of Phineas Dredmoore. It was the only grave marker I knew by name. The only one Mama had ever told me about. It stood high above all the others. It was big enough that I could see it from my bedroom window: Phineas Dredmoore on horseback, an enormous stone bat perched on his arm, its wings spread wide as if it was about to take flight. Mama told me that Phineas was my great-great-great grandpa. He and his wife, Cordelia, had come over from England a hundred some-odd years ago and settled Dredmoore Hollow. They'd come to escape some kind of trouble–bad blood in the family, if I got the story right. Mama was disinclined to talk about it. She seemed to think fondly of Phineas and Cordelia, but she wouldn't say a word about the rest of them. She said it's improper to speak ill of the dead. We had a needlepoint sampler up over the Victrola phonograph with an inscription from Phineas's gravestone:

Some Things You Choose.
Some Things Choose You.

The hooded man grabbed hold of his wheelbarrow again, then bent down and spoke to the wolf.

"You stay put, Jack. Them two jezebels said there's a trap waitin'. 'Burrowin' Ravenweed' they called it, or some such. Anything they're mixed up in, you know it's bad business." The wolf let out a dejected whine and threw himself down on the grass.

The man rolled the wheelbarrow into the graveyard and headed toward the statue of Phineas Dredmoore. He moved slow as a snail, tiptoeing across the witchgrass like he was sneaking up on somebody. He set down the wheelbarrow next to the statue, quiet and gentle as he could. Then he stood up, ran a sleeve over his forehead, and let out a big breath. He reached under his coat. Lightning flashed off a steel ax head. For a second, I thought he was going to chop up the statue. But instead, he picked up the lantern and started to back away, slow and easy, the same way he came in. Once he stood twenty or so paces from the grave, he set down the lantern. Then he tossed the ax high into the air. It hit the ground with a dull thud.

A second later the grass erupted in a fierce explosion, nearly knocking me out of the tree.

I muffled a scream. All around the statue, black vines shot into the sky. They burst up through the ground like cannon shot, sending a blast of dirt and sod across the graveyard. A riotous fluttering filled the air. Great, raggedy wings grew from the vines, black as ravens'. And at the topmost end of each shoot was a set of black claws. The vines slashed at the sky like bullwhips. They snapped branches off trees all around the cemetery and sent the wheelbarrow tumbling across the witchgrass.

The sight was so frightful that I lost my hold on the tree and started to fall. Lucky for me, my shirt caught on a snag. For a couple minutes, I hung there from my shirttail like a bug caught in a spiderweb. Beastly vines scratched and slithered their way across the tombstones below me. I was too petrified to move. Then I clenched my teeth and pulled myself back up onto the limb.

The hooded man was plenty shook up, too. By the time I got myself situated in the tree again, he'd snatched up his lantern and ducked behind a tombstone. He pulled another hatchet out from under his coat and crouched in the shadows, motionless.

After a while, the vines calmed down a bit. The black wings slowed their beating. The claws stopped slashing. They seemed to be waiting for something to move. I held my breath and tried not to think about the branch that was jabbing into my ribs.

The man pulled a strange-looking pipe out of his coat pocket. He edged his way out from behind the tombstone, fumbling to get the pipe up to his lips. Then he blew hard on the mouthpiece, and a queer ghostly sound filled the air— like the howl of winter wind. A churning smoke cloud rose out of the pipe. It seemed impossible; there was so much smoke. You'd have thought the woods were on fire, if it wasn't for the color—an eerie, glowing blue.

Suddenly, the air turned bitter cold. My rain-soaked shirt was like ice against my skin. A flash of lightning lit up the graveyard, and I saw that it was snowing. Silvery sleet poured from the smoke cloud, sending the claw-tipped vines into a fury. Claws slashed at the air. Wings battered violently, whipping the sleet into a blizzard.

It was all I could do to cling to the tree limb. I closed

my eyes against the pelting hailstones. The tree bark turned to ice beneath my cheek.

Little by little, the blizzard subsided. The wings were beating slower and slower. The claw-tipped vines bobbed in the air, heavy and sluggish. They wove back and forth a couple times more, as if trying to shake off the cold. Then they sunk to the ground and went still.

The graveyard fell silent. My heart was pounding so hard it shook my whole body. My fingers hurt from clutching the oak limb.

The hooded man slowly lowered the pipe from his mouth and stared at the frozen vines. "So that's Burrowin' Ravenweed. I don't know about you, Jack, but I've had about enough of this devilry."

Jack the wolf stood in the open gate with his fangs bared and his tail tucked between his legs.

"Let's get what we come for and get out of this place."

Nervous and whimpering, the wolf lumbered up to his side. The man gathered up his wheelbarrow and spade. Then he set the lantern just below Phineas Dredmoore's outstretched arm and set to digging.

"Stay close, Jack," he said. "There might be more of that Ravenweed out where the sod's not frozen."

The wolf snuggled up to the back of his master's legs, a great trembling mountain of fur. A frightful thought occurred to me. I'd run across the graveyard myself just a few minutes ago with no idea what lay hiding under the grass. I'd never heard of anything like that Burrowing Ravenweed in all my life, no matter that I'd read *Hodgeworth's Encyclopedia of Natural Science* cover to cover at least twice. Who ever heard of a vine that had wings and claws?

The man kept on digging, fast and hard. He was plenty liberal with the cusswords, too. I wasn't sure whether I wanted to watch or not, for fear of what he might pull up out of that hole. I had no particular desire to see the bones of my great-great-great grandpa Phineas come unearthed. But I couldn't help myself. My eyes were fixed on the ground.

I clung to my tree limb, hardly breathing.

The man had dug six or so feet into the dirt when a steely noise rang out. He lifted the lantern out of the hole and worked the dirt more carefully now, picking his way around the edges of something solid.

Neither the noise nor the shape made much sense to me. A pine casket would've gone to the worms after a hundred years. But the sound from his spade was metal on metal. Had they buried my great-great-great grandpa in a cast-iron tub?

Now the hooded man got down on his hands and knees, dropping out of my sight in the shadow of the hole. When he stood up again, he was holding a burlap sack stuffed full of something big and solid. There was no clear shape to the thing. It could've been just about anything. The man disappeared into the hole again and came out with another sack, about the same size as the first. He did this three more times, making for five burlap sacks in all, each filled with something odd-shaped and heavy.

He loaded the whole lot into the wheelbarrow and whistled.

"C'mon, Jack. We'd best get out of this godforsaken place before that *thing* thaws out."

He set the lantern on top of his load, spun the wheelbarrow around, and headed out of the gate.

"Confound it!" he muttered, setting the wheelbarrow down. "Forgot the spade."

He hurried back to the hole and jumped down into the darkness. He gave the spade a toss and clambered out again. It landed tip-down, right in front of a gravestone shaped like a winged fish.

The man hurried over to fetch the spade, and just as he did, the ground erupted. A thick shoot of Ravenweed bolted up through the sod and slashed down at him. He sprang toward the gate with uncommon speed for a man of his proportions. Even so, a black claw caught him across the hand. He let out a cry of pain. From my perch in the tree, I let out a shriek of my own, just at the sight of it.

The man dropped to the ground on the other side of the gate, grasping the hurt hand in his good one. He rolled around on the witchgrass, moaning and cursing like a man bewitched. A coil of black smoke rose from his coat sleeve. The wolf ran circles 'round him, whimpering helplessly and snapping at empty air.

After some time, the man finally steadied himself and rose to his knees, shaking and groaning. He raised his left arm and stared at it. It looked to me as if his hand was gone. There was something dark and wispy at the end of his arm, like tufts of fur or feathers. The man stared at his empty coat sleeve, frozen with horror.

It took Mama the better part of an hour to get me out from under her and Poppers' box springs. I sat on their bed, curled up in a quilt, and told the story just like it happened. Poppers snorted through the whole thing. Mama listened without so much as a word while she dabbed comfrey butter on my scratches. I was scraped up head to toe from crawling through the briars, which is how I got out of the graveyard. I jumped from the dead oak clean over the cemetery fence and into the blackberry thicket. A few prickerbush cuts were a long shot better than getting chewed up by that man-eating Ravenweed.

When I was all done, Poppers gave a big yawn and rolled over.

"I'm sure there's a sensible explanation," he said. "Taking into account the dark and the lightning and your overactive imagination."

Mama ignored him. She sat there on the bed, staring off into nowhere, pale and silent. She had a look in her eyes that put my stomach in knots. I'd never seen her act like that before. She never got rattled over anything. In fact, the only thing that ever bothered her at all was Poppers' know-it-all comments.

"Who do you think he was, Mama?" I asked. "Why would he be digging in the Dredmoore family graveyard?"

"I don't know, Eli," she said quietly, still lost in thought.

"Kind of funny that your mama and I never heard any truck," muttered Poppers, pulling the blankets up over his head.

"And what was that . . . that *Ravenweed* thing?" I asked. "It wasn't natural. . . . Things like that just don't exist."

"No, sir, they don't," said Poppers, from under the blankets. "Unless a boy reads too many Tom Swift books, of course."

Mama shot a mean look at the lump in the quilts. Poppers started snoring.

She stood up and peered out the window, wringing her hands. She paced across the room a couple times, a troubled look casting a shadow over her face. Then she sat down next to me again and took a breath. "There's something I need to tell you, Elijah. I've been putting it off for a long time, because . . . well . . . you know how you like to *worry*. But you're old enough now . . . and you've got a right to know."

I nodded blankly. The look on her face did nothing to help calm my jitters. She forced a smile and took hold of my hand.

"I don't suppose tonight's the right time, though," she said. "It's probably best left for morning."

"Is it . . . something about that man in the graveyard?" I asked. "Or the Ravenweed?"

She kissed me on the forehead and flicked my nose. "It's nothing you need to worry about tonight."

Then she gave me a long, tight hug and shoved me toward my bedroom.

I checked my lantern to make sure it had enough kerosene and set it on the bed stand. Despite the knot in my stomach from the night's events, I couldn't help but steal one last peek out the window. Like a fly drawn to candlelight.

Mama's words hung in my mind—*you're old enough now . . . you've got a right to know.*

What did she have to tell me that needed to wait till daylight?

I pulled the shade away from the window just a crack . . . and what I saw knocked the wind right out of me.

There was a dark figure headed across the barnyard with nothing but a dim lantern and a walking stick. The person was headed straight for the old wagon road in a blazing hurry.

I was about to call out for Poppers when a flash of lightning lit up the valley. I had to hold back a holler.

The dark figure was the spitting image of Mama . . . moving fast and fearless toward the Dredmoore family graveyard.

3

A Strange Hour for Company

FOR THE NEXT TWO WEEKS, I WAS JUMPY AS A wild barn cat. I hardly dared to leave the house. I slept in my corduroy knickers, with the lantern on. There was a loaded slingshot tucked under my suspenders day and night, for whatever good that would do.

Burrowing Ravenweed haunted my sleep—and my waking hours, too. I imagined how it would tunnel out of the graveyard and slither its way down to the house. Once it got to the front stoop, it would burst up through the grass, fluttering those ratty black wings. Then it would grope for the side of the house, black claws scratching at the clapboards, feeling their way up the porch rails, up the corner post and onto the roof . . . searching, searching, searching for my window. . . .

I spent many a day pawing through books at the Chester Banks Memorial Library. But I never came across anything that offered any explanations.

Mama kept putting off the chat we were supposed to have—whatever it was she'd wanted to tell me that night of the hooded man and the Ravenweed. She became quiet and serious most of the time, as if nagged by some worry. It was an unsettling change—she was usually so carefree and chatty.

The June rains slogged on past with no sign of anything strange. Midsummer rolled in, sunny and peaceful, and I went back to my regular pastimes. I worked on my squash garden, hoping to grow a prizewinner in time for the Beanbridge Fair. I helped Jeb and Cora Washburn build a retractable rope ladder up to their tree house. And I spent many an afternoon sprawled out in the shade with the new Tom Swift adventure, *Tom Swift Circling the Globe*.

The more I thought about it, the more I wondered whether Poppers was right about that night. Maybe I'd gotten myself so worked up I imagined the whole thing—the hooded man, the hunchback wolf, even the Burrowing Ravenweed. I'd read about folks who would go out walking in their sleep—somnambulists, they're called—and they might dream they're doing just about anything. Could be I'd just gotten myself over-exhausted and somnambulated all the way out to the Dredmoore family graveyard, where I had a bad run-in with the blackberry bushes.

Could be. Anything was possible.

The human mind is a universe of mysteries. (That's what *Hodgeworth's Encyclopedia* says on the subject.)

Things had been quiet and normal ever since, so I did my best to forget about it.

Then one night I was lying in bed, pawing through a smack-dandy book about aerodynamics. My eyes were getting all bleary, and my head was going groggy, and my skin felt all tingly and hot from getting sunburned out in the garden. My bed felt so nestish and cozy, it was all I could do to stay awake. So I changed into my union suit, tucked my slingshot under the pillow, and I was just reaching over to snuff out the hurricane lantern . . .

When all of a sudden, the crickets went quiet.

The wind went still.

A strange chill came over the air.

The growl of a motor echoed across the valley. The crunch of gravel under tires. Someone was driving up the hill toward our house.

I went clammy as a trout.

Out in the barnyard, Dandy and Bloomers set to lowing. Mr. Plinkett's coon dog howled like a lost soul. And every chicken in the whole valley got to clucking. I was just about to bolt for Mama and Poppers' room, across the hall, when a knock came on the front door.

I cracked open my bedroom door right as Poppers started down the stairs in his nightshirt.

"Who the devil could be calling at this hour of the night?" he mumbled, half asleep. He slapped at the front of his nightshirt, searching for his pocket watch.

He opened the front door and a tall blonde lady

came shooting into the house. She threw her arms around Poppers' neck and nearly knocked him off his feet. I'd never seen such a pretty gal in all my life. She was wearing a snazzy red dress and gloves, with a fox fur wrap around her shoulders and a fur hat to match. She was still smooching Poppers all over both cheeks, when in came a second gal. This one was dressed all in black, from her high-heeled boots all the way up to the lacy hat perched on top of her hair, which was whirled up high in the air like a tornado. She stood in the doorway, clutching a black parasol–it was closed up tight and pointed in front of her like a sword.

"You must be Horace!" cried the one in the fox wrap. The fox's head bobbed up and down almost as if it was sniffing Poppers over.

"How wonderful it is to see you all!" said the one with the cyclone hairdo. Her eyes were purplish blue. She pasted on a smile that looked like she was in mortal pain.

"We're your sisters-in-law," said the first one. "I'm Serena and this is Agnes. I'm sure Katrina's told you all about us."

Poppers stood there speechless in his flannel nightshirt. He had red lipstick marks all over his face and neck.

Mama plodded down the stairs in her nightgown and wool stockings. I snuck along behind her.

"Serena?" she said. Her face went pale. "Agnes? What are you–"

"Katrina!" squealed the one in the fox fur, the one called Serena. She threw both arms around Mama, who stood stiff as a plank with a stunned look on her face. I thought I saw the fox curl its lip back in a snarl. I blinked and decided I'd been seeing things.

The other one, Agnes, grabbed hold of Mama's hand and shook it hard, fluttering her eyelashes and smiling for all she was worth. When she stepped away, she planted the tip of her parasol into the floor with such force it left a puncture mark.

"It's been far too long!" said Serena. She held Mama at arm's length and studied her over. "Agnes and I have missed you desperately. Haven't we, Aggie?"

Agnes nodded so hard it's a wonder she didn't wrench her neck. "How wonderful it is to see you all!" she said for the second time.

She flashed those purple eyes at me and Poppers. They could cut right through you. We looked at each other like we'd each swallowed a live crawfish. Then we stared at Mama.

"Kat?" said Poppers. "Are these ladies your sisters?"

Mama nodded, but just barely. She'd been stunned silent from the moment the door swung open. Good reason, too. Mama hadn't spoken to her sisters since before I was born. They'd cut ties way back before Mama had even met Poppers. There'd been some kind of family squabble. Mama would never talk about it—not to me or my father or anyone else that I knew of—so I knew it must've been a bad one. The only thing I knew about the quarrel was that Mama and Grandma Ester came out on one side, and almost everybody else was on the other. Now and then we got a letter or a package from one of the Dredmoore relatives. But before Poppers and I could get a look at it, Mama would toss it in the woodstove. Unopened. It was unusual behavior for Mama. Whenever somebody so much as mentioned Dredmoores, she'd go ice-cold snippy and change the subject.

It seemed a genuine marvel that these two fancy ladies were my aunts, especially the chatty one, Serena. They looked like those gussied-up girls you see in the Sears Roebuck catalog, showing off expensive outfits. Not a thing like my mother, who was kind of short and plump and had frizzy hair with a few sprouts of gray in it. She favored union suits and flannel shirts, and she didn't have a lump of make-up to her name.

"Well now!" said Serena, stepping toward me with a flirty smile. "This must be our nephew, Ezekial."

"Elijah," I said. My voice cracked.

Her teeth were shiny white and perfect, all except for a little sharp one on top that bit into her bottom lip when she smiled.

"Let me just look at you!" she said.

She stepped up and grabbed my face with both hands. She studied me over something serious. Agnes nudged up beside her and did the same. Both of them seemed especially focused on my chin. It was awkward strange, but I weathered it out.

"He's got the Dredmoore blood, all right," declared Serena. "Handsomest boy I've ever seen."

"True marvel of nature," said Agnes in a flat tone.

"You must be about twelve?" asked Serena.

"In a few months," I said, kind of pleased they were taking such an interest.

"Then I don't suppose you've . . . started shaving yet?" asked Serena delicately.

"Shucks, no!" I laughed. "Not for a few years, I bet."

The sisters looked at each other, a twinkle in their eyes. I couldn't imagine why they'd care about such a thing.

"Of course not," said Serena with a chuckle. "Your silly old aunts don't know the first thing about young men."

Agnes drew a pocket watch out of her parasol and stole a peek. She looked bored. It seemed to me that Serena was the one in charge, and Agnes was stuck with second fiddle. Without the high-heeled shoes and the tornado hairdo, she would've been a full head shorter than her sister.

They both turned to Mama.

"Katrina, I'll be blunt about it," said Serena. "We've come to make amends."

Agnes nodded, her face strained into a sort of pout. "There are no words to express our regret," she said.

"Fifteen years is too long to hold a grudge," Serena went on. "We've changed our ways, Katrina. You'd hardly know us now. We completely gave up all the *you know what*. We figured it was time we came by to patch things up and meet our clever brother-in-law, Horace. And our handsome nephew, Elias."

"Elijah," I corrected her again. But she didn't seem to hear me.

"We sure would like to put everything behind us," said Serena, "and be family again."

"One big, happy family," said Agnes, her eyes glassed over.

I wondered if she wasn't a tiny bit addled in the head. Truth be told, they both seemed a little peculiar.

Mama glanced back and forth between the two of them with an anxious expression on her face. I'd never seen her so shook up. She looked like she was trying to work out what to say but was coming up blank.

Poppers decided to break the silence. "Now, I'm sure whatever went on between you gals all those years ago–"

But Mama cut him off.

"Horace." She took Poppers' hand and gave it a pat. "How about you and Eli go fix some hot cider for everyone?"

"Well . . . sure, I guess, Kat, but–"

"My sisters and I have some things to talk over," said Mama.

Me and Poppers stared at her.

"Just us ladies," said Mama. "I'll call you when we're finished."

Poppers gave her a whipped-puppy scowl and shuffled off to the kitchen. I followed after him, and as soon as the door was shut, I put my ear up to the keyhole. Poppers threw a washrag at me and told me to mind my own business. I could see he was steamed. He always liked to be the expert on everything; he hated to get left out. He grumbled under his breath while he jabbed a fire poker at the coals in the cookstove. Outside, the rain went *wap-wap-wap*, hard as pebbles against the kitchen window.

Mama and her sisters were out there a good hour before they hollered for us to bring in the cider. Agnes and Serena were all smiley like everything was fine and dandy. But Mama had a firm set to her jaw. I didn't know what to make of it.

"It truly was nice to see you folks after all these long years," said Serena. "Agnes and I best get going now. It's a long drive back. And this damp weather does the devil to Sister's allergies."

Agnes sniffed at the hot cider as if she expected it to be rancid, then pushed it away with the tip of her parasol. Serena gave her a nudge. She startled and let out a tremendous sneeze.

"Nonsense!" said Poppers. "This time of night? And poor Agnes on her deathbed with allergies?"

"Don't you worry about us," said Serena. "If we have too hard a time, we'll just pull over and sleep in the Franklin."

Agnes let out another sneeze.

"No kin of ours is sleeping in any infernal automobile!" said Poppers. "Not when we've got a spare room just sitting there empty and all–"

"Now, Horace . . . ," Mama broke in.

"–all set up with bedspreads and everything!" Poppers went on. "We keep it ready for Grandma Ester."

"Oh, we couldn't intrude in such a way!" said Serena. Her fox wrap seemed to gaze at Mama with pleading eyes.

"You're family!" said Poppers. He turned to Mama. "Right, Kat?"

Mama sighed and nodded. She didn't look too happy with the notion.

"I'll put out some clean linens," she said, and headed off for the upstairs closet.

Poppers and I stood there for a while grinning dumbly at my aunts. Serena didn't look the least bit surprised to be staying. There was no question they had some odd ways—what with Serena's overdone cheerfulness and Agnes running a few apples short of a bushel. But that couldn't be why Mama cut ties with them. Whatever had happened all those years back must've been a pretty big deal. It wasn't like Mama to hold a grudge for so long. I watched my aunts pace around the sitting room, ogling the needlepoint samplers, poking the Victrola, and plunking the piano keys.

On the one hand, it was good to see that Agnes and Serena wanted to put things right with Mama and the rest of us. On the other hand, they sure had picked a strange hour of the night to do it.

4

Grandma Gone Missing

FOR SOME REASON OR OTHER, THE ROOSTER missed his cock-a-doodle-doos the next morning. I didn't wake up till the sun was shining straight into my eyes. I pulled on my Sunday knickerbockers and hurried downstairs, hoping I hadn't missed anything.

"Well, look who's up!" said Serena. "I hope you've got an appetite this morning. Your Auntie Agnes and I have been putting out quite a spread. It's not every day we get to have breakfast with our favorite nephew."

Agnes was sitting by the kitchen stove, gazing into a tiny mirror. She pulled a toothy comb out of her parasol and used it to tidy up her cyclone hairdo. I could smell hot griddle cakes and bacon.

"Your folks said they'd be back shortly," said Serena. "They went down to your neighbors' place. Sounded like some sort of emergency."

They were both wearing lacy pink aprons over their

outfits–Agnes's was inside out. Serena had that beady-eyed fox fur wrapped around her shoulders again. Its eyes seemed to follow me around the room.

"They went down to Plinketts'?" I stole a look out the window. Mr. Plinkett's black Ford truck was gone. "Did they say what *kind* of emergency?"

"I don't believe they did," said Serena. She turned to Agnes. "Did you hear what the matter was, Sister?"

Agnes was still peering into the little mirror, plucking her eyebrows. She shook her head.

Serena put an arm around me and guided me toward the kitchen table. "I'm sure it's nothing to worry about, Uriah."

"Elijah," I corrected her.

"Besides, this gives us a chance to get to know each other!"

She stepped up behind her sister and snatched the mirror out of her hand. They gave each other a dark look. Then Agnes got up and smiled at me, batting her eyelashes.

"Would you like some pancakes, Nephew?" she asked.

"Um . . . all right," I said. Serena shoved a chair up behind me.

The whole thing gave me an uneasy feeling. It wasn't like Mama and Poppers to race off without a word–especially not the both of them at once–no matter what the problem was. And my aunts seemed entirely unconcerned about the situation.

Serena crinkled her nose.

Agnes slung her parasol over her arm and went to the

cookstove. She stared at the griddle like it was some kind of complicated machine. Then she tried to scoop up a burnt flapjack with a carving knife. The pancake slipped off the blade, so she grabbed the steaming pan with her bare hand. She let out a howl–

"Thundercrack!"

A blast of sparks shot into the air, and the griddle busted to pieces with a thunderous boom. Hotcakes flew in all directions. Agnes sprang back from the stove, waving her parasol at the smoke. She stuck her burnt fingers in her mouth and gazed over at her sister in horror.

"My goodness, Sister!" Serena let out a nervous chuckle. "You must've overheated that griddle something frightful."

Serena grabbed hold of my hand. "I hope you won't think poorly of your old aunties. We're not much use in the kitchen, I'm afraid. I don't imagine we'll be invited back if we keep busting up the cookery."

The floor was smattered with chunks of griddle and smoldering hotcakes. I tried to act like it was no big deal–as if frying pans overheated and blew to pieces every day at our place. And another thing that seemed strange: where had Agnes got such a strange cussword as *Thundercrack*?

Some time later, Agnes wrestled a half dozen pancakes off the stove. She plopped them down in front of me, alongside a cup of cider. Two black feathers–like the ones in her hat– floated in the juice. Serena sat across from me with a big grin on her face, watching me. The only way I could get those flapjacks down was to smother every piece in crab-apple jam and swallow without chewing.

Both Agnes and Serena kept stealing peaks out the window like they hoped Mama and Poppers would hurry up and get home. I was hoping for the very same thing. These new aunts of mine were plenty nice, no question about that–a little *too* nice. I would've thought they were putting me on somehow. But why? They'd never even met me before.

"One of these days you'll have to come up to our place for a visit," said Serena. She shoveled another flapjack onto my plate. "You'd like it there. I can already tell. Sister and I were admiring your squash garden this morning. We truly wish we had your touch at agriculture. We're both uncommonly fond of gardening, but we don't begin to have your gift for it. If I had to guess, you're raising those butternut squash to show at the county fair."

"Yes'm," I said, struggling to swallow another mouthful of hotcakes. They tasted like damp sawdust. "Last year I won second prize."

"Didn't I tell you, Sister?" crowed Serena.

Agnes was busy sweeping busted griddle and hotcakes off the floor.

Serena leaned across the table and put her hand on my arm. She was wearing the same red gloves as the night before.

"The reason Agnes and I like gardening so much," she said, "is because we're both exceedingly fascinated with the natural sciences–plants, animals, astronomy, and so forth."

I nodded obligingly. It was hard to picture either one of them sitting down with *Hodgeworth's Encyclopedia*, never mind out collecting dung beetles and damselflies for their insect collections. I thought I saw the fox wrap open one eye and steal a peek at me. That thing gave me the spooks.

"You know what I've always been meaning to do?" Serena went on. "I've always meant to build myself one of those crystal radios that are so popular with the young folks these days. One of the big ones with copper wire that you run all over your ceiling. Have you ever seen one of those?"

I washed down a rubbery hunk of flapjack and looked up to see if she was serious. "Sure . . ." I said. "I've got a bunch of crystal radios up in my room. I make my own batteries out of cobbler's nails, salt water, and–"

"Yes, indeed," Serena cut in. "But you know what I like most of all? A good book! Isn't that so, Agnes?"

Agnes snorted and swept a pile of flapjack crumbs under the butter churn.

"Sister and I are both reading Tom Swift books just now," chirped Serena. "It's infernally hard to set them aside! Marvelous stories, if you're fond of adventure tales as I am. You haven't read any of the Tom Swift books, have you, Elijah?"

"Yes'm . . . they're my favorite," I said. Was she pulling my leg with all this talk about crystal radios and Tom Swift stories? I supposed I ought to be thankful that she finally got my name right, at least.

Just then, someone knocked on the door. Agnes spun around with a relieved look on her face.

"I wonder who that could be," said Serena. "Were you expecting visitors, Elijah?"

I shook my head and got up to open the door.

It was Mr. Plinkett. I nearly jumped out of my boots, I was so happy to see him. I snuck a look out the door, hoping to see Mama and Poppers fetching things out of Mr. Plinkett's truck. But there was no one else.

"G'morning, Mr. Plinkett," I said, trying not to sound too anxious. "Are my folks still down at your place?"

He stood teetering on the porch, gazing straight ahead. He didn't seem to see me. His mustache twitched every few seconds, as if he had an itch. What's more, he had a bad case of the hiccups.

"Mr. Plinkett?" I said. "Are . . . are you all right?"

He hiccuped again.

After some time, Serena stepped up beside me. "Can we help you with something, sir?"

Agnes rapped the floor hard with the tip of her parasol.

"Oh . . . yes . . . yes, indeed," said Mr. Plinkett, staring off into nowhere. He let out another hiccup. "Got a letter . . . for Elijah . . . from your Ma and Pa."

He pulled a letter out of his overalls and held it straight out in front of him. I stared at it a moment, confused.

"A letter from Elijah's parents?" said Serena. "Now, why in the world . . . ?"

I reached up and took the envelope. Mr. Plinkett held

on to it so tight, it was all I could do to pry it out of his fingers.

"I don't understand," I said, tearing it open. "I thought they just went down to your place?"

He stood there dazed for a minute, twitching his mustache. Then he hiccuped once more and wobbled back to his truck and drove off. Something was wrong. *Very* wrong. Why would Mr. Plinkett act so odd? He was usually so gabby you couldn't get a word in edgewise.

The letter was written in Mama's chicken-scratch handwriting:

Dear Elijah,

Sorry we didn't wake you to say good-bye. We got an emergency telegram last night from Hattie Crackens, that neighbor friend of your Grandma Ester's. She said that Grandma has been acting odd lately, and last night she flew off in her hot-air balloon. It's our guess that she's headed up north to see Great Uncle Ezra in Canada like she's always talking about. We made arrangements with the Plinketts to watch the farm while we go after Grandma. You can go stay with your aunts, if they will have you. Make sure you are on your best behavior. We should be back before you know it.

Obey your aunts no matter what!

All our love,

M & P

"Goodness!" said Serena, peering over my shoulder. "Poor Grandma Ester! I wish your mama had woken us. We would've gladly gone and looked for her ourselves." She turned to Agnes and shook her head. "Isn't that just like Katrina? Always the one to sacrifice for the good of others."

Agnes nodded stiffly. "A perfect saint."

"And, of course, you're welcome to come stay at our place, Elijah," said Serena. "It's the least we can do now that we're all family again. Long overdue, in my opinion. I'm sure your folks will be back in no time. They'll probably want to come up and stay with us for a few days themselves."

"Well," said Agnes, "we might as well get going then."

She yanked the apron off her shoulders and shoved the dirty dishes into the sink with a sweep of her parasol.

Serena let out a woeful sigh. "I suppose you're right, Sister. There's no point sitting around here and worrying our heads off about poor Grandma Ester. Elijah, why don't you put a couple pairs of knickers in a sack, and we'll head off to our place while there's plenty of daylight to burn, hmm?"

I didn't know what to say. My head was reeling. It all seemed too much, too fast, too hard to make sense of. It was true that Grandma Ester was prone to crazy adventures. But she hadn't gone anywhere in her hot-air balloon since before I was born. Not that I'd heard about, anyhow. As far as I knew, she kept it stored away in her horse barn and only took it out on the Fourth of July–and even then, she always tethered it to a fence post. It wasn't like Mama and Poppers to go off in a whirlwind and hunt for her, either. In fact, I'd always got the impression that Grandma Ester could take care of herself as good as anybody.

Serena gazed down at me with an expression of grave pity. Agnes tapped the floor impatiently with the tip of her parasol.

What else could I do? I packed up some clothes, a few Tom Swift books, and a crystal radio. Then I went to the bed stand to see what my trouble-bug thought of the trip. Jonah was hiding under a half-eaten cabbage leaf, curled up and quivering. I gave him a nudge. He let out a ghastly peep and burrowed deep into the moss as fast as he could go. This seemed like an ominous sign to me—if only Grandma Ester had been there to decipher it.

I wondered if I should try to wriggle my way out of the trip? Maybe I could get the Plinketts to take me in until Mama and Poppers got back.

I tapped Jonah's house. Complete silence.

Could be I was getting carried away again . . . getting worked up over nothing. Last time Jonah burrowed into the moss like this he just molted out of his fur and turned from purple to brown.

Maybe that's all it was.

I put the lid on his tin house and set it back on the bed stand, figuring it was best to leave him be. Then I dragged my carpetbag outside, climbed into my aunts' great big Franklin automobile, and off we went.

Just as we turned onto the county road, I saw a flatbed

truck pull off the shoulder and head up the valley toward our place. A shiver shot up my backbone. It looked an awful lot like that truck I'd seen the hooded man driving the night of the Ravenweed. I peered out the back window and saw a big crate roped down on the back. That settled my nerves a bit. It was most likely some new piece of milking equipment headed up to the Plinkett farm. Unlike Poppers, Mr. Plinkett was big on making things modern.

I leaned back against the seat and listened to the road rumble underneath our tires. Agnes turned and glanced over the seat at me with those icy, purple eyes. This time she wasn't smiling.

5

Moaning Marsh

EVER SINCE MR. PLINKETT DROVE HOME WITH his 1924 black Ford truck, I'd been after Poppers to buy us an automobile. That truck was the most wondrous mechanical thing I'd ever seen. It had an internal combustion engine, not steam powered like those old Stanley motorcars. A true miracle of modern science. I wanted Poppers to get an automobile more than anything in the whole world.

That is, until I rode in my aunts' Franklin.

It was a thing of beauty, that car–shiny red and long as a train engine, with a flashy silver grille, a solid roof, and headlights the size of dinner plates.

But it was a chariot of terror once Serena got behind the wheel. She was in an all-fire hurry, sailing over rut holes and around gravel corners like we were in a derby race. Half the time we had two wheels in the gutter. People were never meant to move at such a jaw-rattling speed. What if a tire came off? What if we plowed headlong into a tree? I clung to the seat cushion for all I was worth and tried not to look out the window.

We spent the better part of the day weaving around on back roads, tempting death at every bend. We climbed deeper and deeper into the hills. Each road got more scrawny and ragged than the last.

Even worse than the driving was Agnes's change of disposition. She'd gone stone silent and sour the minute we left Dredmoore Hollow. After a couple hours, I asked how far it was to their place. But the only thing I got back was a squinty glare.

All in all, the day's events had left me hollowed out and numb. I wondered if these long-lost aunts of mine were up to something. But I couldn't figure what. I'd seen the letter written in Mama's own handwriting, no question about it. And Mr. Plinkett was Poppers' oldest friend—he was as trustworthy as they come. Though he certainly had acted strange that morning. . . .

The sun was starting to set when we came to a crossroads with a pair of crooked road signs. The one pointing left said:

Blossom Springs—6 Miles

I was mortally thankful to see we'd finally closed in on a town. The name had a comforting ring to it, too—Blossom Springs. You could picture meadows full of goldenrod and sunshine, butterflies fluttering on the breeze.

Then I noticed the sign pointing to the right. It was weathered gray and draped in raggedy moss. The words looked like they'd been carved out with a hot poker:

Moaning Marsh
Dead En

Moaning Marsh? What kind of a name was that? The sound of it put my hair on end. I supposed that last part was meant to say *Dead End* but the *d* had worn off. Grandma Ester would've called it a bad omen.

I bit my lip and prayed. But my luck was sour as always and Serena wheeled the car to the right. The road turned to a narrow rut and began snaking its way up a steep hill. Half-dead trees clung to the slope. The track was nearly washed out on every corner. I grabbed on to the back of Agnes's seat, and she turned around with a scowl that all but pried my fingers loose.

"Not far now," said Serena in a merry tone. She hadn't spoken to me for the past three hours, so it surprised me to hear her voice all of a sudden. The fox wrap fixed its tiny black eyes on me over her shoulder. I tried not to look at it.

The farther up the hill we went, the more sickly the trees looked, growing paler and paler till they were the color of bones. Tree skeletons is what they were. Dead, half-toppled things with broken-off branches.

The sun had nearly set by the time the Franklin lurched over the last ridge. My breath went still.

Damp air and dead trees closed in around us–gnarled-up and rotten with moss beards hanging off their limbs. Vines and tangle brush filled every inch of space, choking out the last glimmer of evening light. I shut my eyes tight and tried to think about my favorite fishing hole up on Six-Mile Brook.

But it was no use.

Branches and wet leaves slapped at the Franklin's windows as we slogged down the lane. Between the falling darkness and the mist seeping out of the bog, I couldn't see the road at all now. If not for the *slup-slup-slup* of the wheels bumping over muddy ruts, I would've thought we were driving on top of nothing but bog water.

After an infernally long time, the forest opened up and the road meandered into open marsh. Scraggly little swamp oaks grew on either side of us–they swayed wildly as we rumbled past. The track bristled with their sharp little stumps, as if someone had only recently carved a path through. A short ways ahead, a grassy hill rose up out of the bog. It looked as if it had been dropped there out of the sky. In the dimming light, I could make out a cockeyed old house and barn sitting at the very top of the hill. They were nearly as rundown and creepy as the bog.

A lump stuck in my throat as we slogged toward them. *No way that could be my aunts' house. Impossible.* Two fancy gals like Serena and Agnes? Frilly dresses and high-heeled shoes? Gussied-up hairdos and perfume? Why would they hole away out in the middle of this gloomy swamp?

The Franklin growled its way up the grassy hill. A

moment later, we rolled through an old whitewashed gate. A big sign hung overhead:

THE MAGIC SNIPPERS
Beauty Salon
Serena & Agnes Dredmoore, Proprietors
Est. 1922

Serena pulled up in front of the house and brought the Franklin to a stop by slamming into a half-burnt tree stump.

"Well," she chirped, "wasn't that a nice drive?"

My fingers hurt from clinging to the seat cushion.

Off in the valley beyond, the lights of a little town twinkled away–Blossom Springs, I reckoned. I'd have given anything to be down there.

There was a barber pole stuck into the ground next to the barn, and another Magic Snippers sign nailed up onto the barn boards. The door had been torn off some other building and cobbled on with rusty nails. This sure didn't seem like any kind of place to run a beauty shop. People would have to be out of their heads to drive way out to this swamp for a haircut.

I glanced from the house to the barn, my brain racing for some way I might talk my aunts into taking me back to Dredmoore Hollow.

"It's late," said Agnes, yanking the car door open. "We'll show you straight to your cot."

Straight to my cot?

Had they been planning on me coming here? Or did they just keep a place ready for visitors?

Agnes hooked my arm with the crook of her parasol and dragged me out onto the grass—I barely managed to snatch my carpetbag off the seat. She led me around the side of the house, moving at such a clip that it was all I could do to keep up.

Serena hurried along next to me, yapping away, pleasant as ever. The snout of her fox wrap bobbed up and down like it was sniffing at the foul marsh air.

"You're going to love our guest cottage, Elijah," she said. "It's the sort of place every boy dreams of. You can do as you please down here, with no grown-ups to boss you around." She gave me a conspiring wink.

The air was damp and cold and full of swamp stink.

I thought we were headed for a side door, but Agnes veered away from the house and pulled me down the hill . . . toward the marsh. My skin went prickly with goose bumps. I would've run back to the Franklin if I could've. She had such a tight grip on my arm that it was going numb.

A crooked little shack sat on a hump of grass at the edge of the swamp. I would've taken it to be a woodshed. But the door was painted white and there was a welcome mat on the stoop. The building leaned out toward the swamp like it was ready to fall in.

"Here it is," said Serena. "The guest cottage! It'll be your very own private getaway till your mother and father come to fetch you."

Agnes grabbed a lantern that was hanging off to the side of the door and shoved me through the doorway.

"Now isn't this homey?" said Serena.

There was a cot covered with tatty blankets up against one wall. On top of a wooden crate was a half-melted candle poking out of a sardine tin. The only other things in the room were a bedpan under the cot and a wash bucket full of rust-colored water.

Serena let out a gasp and snatched the lantern out of Agnes's hand. She grabbed hold of my jaw so suddenly that I banged the back of my head against the wall.

"Goodness, Elijah!" she said. "I do believe you've got a bit of swamp rash coming on. You must have the same constitution as me. The marsh air brings it on in such a hurry you won't know what hit you."

"*Swamp rash?*" I reached for my face, but she stopped my hand.

"Don't scratch at it!" she said. "That'll only make it worse."

Agnes handed Serena a bundle of cloth. I had no idea where she'd gotten it. I sure didn't see her carrying it when we came in. Serena opened the bundle and took out a clump of white fluff–it looked like cotton, except it was full of sparkly little flecks that glimmered in the lamplight. A flowery smell filled the room, roses and peppermint mixed together.

Serena breathed a big sigh of relief. "You're in luck, Elijah. Sister and I always try to keep some of our special rash remedy on hand for situations like this."

"I really don't feel any–"

Agnes cut me off with a shout. "Don't touch it, Sister!"

She knocked Serena's hand away from the fluff.

Serena spun around and gave her a furious glare. "No need to worry, Sister. Cousin Japeth assured me that *human touch* won't upset the remedy in the least. It was prepared entirely by our dear friends overseas and tested with excellent success on both of the twins . . . as I'm quite certain I explained to you earlier."

Agnes nodded and let go of Serena's arm. But the look in her eye was a long shot from sisterly affection.

Serena worked the fluff into a lengthy strip. She held one end under my chin, then wrapped it over the top of my head and down again. She got in three or four wraps that way, till I was bundled up like I was ready for winter. I was surprised to find that the stuff felt every bit as good as it smelled–it was the softest, warmest, most wonderful thing I'd ever touched. A cozy, tingly feeling swept through me. Whatever worries I'd had about Moaning Marsh and everything else– none of it bothered me now.

"How does that feel, Elijah? Not too tight, is it?" Serena asked.

I shook my head. It was perfect. Everything was perfect.

"Just dandy," I said with a giggle. "What's it called?"

"Oh, it's an old Dredmoore family remedy." Serena led me over to the cot and settled me onto the blankets. "Lullabeetle Silk. All the old-time farmers use it. It'll cure that swamp rash of yours in no time."

The Witches of Dredmoore Hollow

My mother did keep plenty of old Dredmoore family remedies around the house. She'd dole them out anytime I got sick. But they were mostly foul-tasting tonics or crushed-up herbs. I had to pinch my nose in order to swallow the nasty stuff. If she'd had any Lullabeetle Silk on hand, she'd been keeping it to herself, which seemed like a cruel and selfish thing to do. It was pure heaven against my skin, warm as a campfire and fresh smelling as wild mint.

"Well, Sister and I might as well get off to bed," said Serena. She let out a big yawn. I thought I saw the fox wrap do the same. "It's awful late, and we have a big day ahead of us tomorrow. I'm sure you'll want to explore the marsh, Elijah. There's natural wonders by the dozen."

I nodded agreeably, as best I could wrapped up in lovely Lullabeetle Silk.

"Come along, Sister," she said to Agnes. "I do believe we've exhausted our poor nephew."

Agnes set down the lantern on the crate next to my cot. She turned the light down low, then leaned toward me, glaring with those cold purple eyes.

"You keep that Lullabeetle Silk tight against your chin, you hear?"

"Yes'm," I said. And I meant it. If I had my way, I'd stay wrapped up in that silk forever and ever.

They shut the door, and I heard a lock snap shut from the other side. Something didn't feel right about that—though I couldn't think what at the moment.

I took out a Tom Swift book and read for a while. But the

words swam on the page, and that made my mind wander. So instead, I tinkered with the crystal radio I'd brought along, using my jackknife to tighten the wires. There was no sign of a radio station anywhere on the coil, but I didn't care. Everything seemed so wonderful and interesting with that warm, cozy silk snuggled around my face.

I fell asleep with the radio on my chest and the sound of dead airwaves hissing into the night.

Part 2

Hallucination is the experience of seeing, hearing, feeling, or smelling things that are not real, and occurs most frequently among sufferers of psychotic disorders. Hallucinations may also be prompted by extreme fatigue or anxiety. In one notable case, a farm boy in Schlossburg, Germany, attempted to "herd" the furniture out of his house. He was later observed attempting to milk a rocking chair.

—*Hodgeworth's Encyclopedia of Natural Science*

6

Lullabeetle Silk

I DREAMT I WAS LYING IN A CAVE. IT WAS WARM and peaceful and there was a musical hum coming from somewhere off in the distance. I stared up at the cave ceiling, which was cloudy white and dappled with shadowy movement. A dim light shone through, flickering like a lantern. In the glow, I could see a crisscross of threads, as if the cave was being woven from wool as I watched.

I was thinking how odd it was for a tunnel to be made of stitching yarn, when I noticed that the light was fading. The cave grew dark and close. The only air was my own damp breath. I tried to lift my hand to my face, but it was pinned flat against my chest. I tried to lift my legs, my head . . . I tried to wriggle my shoulders . . . but they were all lashed down.

I was wrapped tight as a mummy.

I couldn't breathe.

In a rush of panic, I tried to wake myself from the

dream . . . and found that I wasn't asleep. Suddenly I remembered the Lullabeetle Silk. I was bound head to toe in the stuff—*a human cocoon.* The sweet, flowery smell had turned musty and sour. I kicked and struggled, but the silk was too strong. The humming sound turned shrill and violent, like the noise of a thousand crazed crickets.

I fought to move my hands enough so I could claw at the wrappings. Something sharp jabbed into my knuckles, and I let out a scream. Then I realized it was only my jackknife.

My jackknife!

I'd fallen asleep while I was working on my radio, and I'd left the knife lying open on my chest. Any other time, I would've been mortified to do such a foolish thing. But given the circumstances, it was a grand stroke of luck. I worked the knife around so I could get hold of the handle. My head was dizzy for want of air. Everything was going black.

I punched my blade through the cocoon. There was a beastly shriek . . . and a burst of cool air. I hacked and slashed at the silk, ripping it from my body in sticky clumps.

Finally, I burst free of the cocoon and tumbled from the cot to the floor. I gasped for air, still clutching my jackknife. I spun around, searching the room, stabbing at the air like a wild man.

Nothing moved. The room was silent. Lullabeetle Silk hung from the cot in tattered cobwebs. In the dim lamplight, I thought I saw a half dozen tiny beetles slip between the floorboards. But when I turned up the lantern, they were gone.

I awoke to the sound of a lock snapping open. A sharp pain shot through my neck. I'd fallen asleep on the shed floor, as far as I could get from the shredded Lullabeetle Silk. I was clutching a stick of kindling with one hand, my jackknife with the other. The door burst open and in rushed Serena and Agnes, both their faces wide eyed and eager.

"How's my favorite nephew this morning?" sang Serena. She stopped cold when she saw the empty cot.

Agnes turned and saw me hunkered in the corner. She pushed her way past Serena and grabbed hold of my jaw. Her face was beet red, and she shook so much I thought her tornado hairdo would topple down on me. She jerked my head around mercilessly as she studied my chin. Then she pushed me away and howled: "He tore off the silk before it could work!" Drops of spit flew from her mouth. "It's *ruined*!"

"It tried to suffocate me!" I cried. "It strapped me to the cot. . . . I couldn't breathe!"

"Fifteen years we've waited for this!" Agnes shrieked. She glared at Serena. "This is your fault. You should've listened to me! We should've tied him to the cot like I said!"

My skin went clammy. *Should've tied me to the cot?*

Serena clutched her sister's arm and backed her into the wall. "Did you check the silk for beetles like I told you?"

Agnes fell silent. The color slowly drained from her face. "I . . . I didn't think we were supposed to touch it on account of–"

Serena cut her off. "The remedy came ready-to-use! Prepared by someone . . . outside the family. What could go wrong? Nothing! All you had to do was check for beetles like I asked. Apparently, even that was too much to expect of you!"

They stared at each other in silence for a while, till finally, Serena took a deep breath and stepped back from her sister. She turned to me, struggling to calm herself.

"Our poor nephew," she said. "You must've suffered a *terrible* nightmare to tear that Lulla' Silk to shreds like you did!"

"It wasn't a nightmare!" My voice quavered. "That . . . stuff was all around me. I couldn't even move!"

Serena chuckled and petted me on the head.

"Well, I'm sure that's what it felt like, Elijah. That's the funny thing about Lullabeetle Silk. Folks will toss and turn in their sleep and get all tangled up in the stuff . . . and you know how remedies can play tricks on the mind. Sister and I really should've warned you."

I glanced over at the cot. Strands of silk jittered in the breeze.

"You and I are a lot alike, Elijah." Serena leaned in close and dropped her voice to a whisper. "Clever people are prone to an excess of imagination. It's nothing to be ashamed of. I've always been afraid of the dark myself. And lightning storms! Goodness, I can't bear the sound of thunder. But a person can't help her disposition, can she?"

I was pretty sure Serena was stretching the truth–she didn't have an anxious bone in her body, as far as I could see. Could be she was just trying to make me feel better. But I knew what had happened with that Lullabeetle Silk, and I sure as shooting had *not* imagined it.

"Don't you worry, Elijah," she said. "We've got plenty of other remedies. No nephew of ours is going to break out in a disfiguring swamp rash. Isn't that so, Sister?"

Agnes nodded, but just barely. She glared at me so fiercely I had to look away.

"Well, I don't know about you two," said Serena, "but I'm starving for a nice breakfast."

Agnes stared at her sister as if she'd lost her mind.

"If the boy is going to stay with us," said Serena, looking Agnes square in the eye, "then he'd ought to help with a few chores."

Agnes's mouth pursed up and twitched as if she'd bitten into something sour. "Might's well, I guess."

"We're all family, aren't we?" Serena crinkled her nose at me. "Everybody has to help out."

She scooped up the blankets and shredded Lullabeetle Silk off the cot and tucked them under her arm.

"D'you know how to cook, boy?" Agnes gave me a doubtful frown. "It'd be fine with me to have somebody other than Grobbs fix a meal for a change."

I nodded. "Yes'm. Mama taught me how to cook just about anything."

"I'll bet she did," said Agnes, sneering. "Everyone's little sweetheart."

My blood went hot to hear her poke at Mama like that.

I wondered what could've happened to turn Agnes so bitter? No doubt it was among the things Mama meant to tell me . . . someday.

"Wonderful!" said Serena. She shoved her sister toward the door. "How about you head over to the chicken coop and fetch some eggs, Elijah? Then you can show us some of that fancy cooking your mama taught you. Hmm?"

"Split some kindling and stoke up the cookstove while you're at it," said Agnes. She knocked the door open with a jab from her parasol. "I don't like my eggs runny. Nor all dried out, either."

"Chicken coop's out back of the barn," added Serena. She took her sister by the arm. "If you see any black eggs, just leave them be. The rooster is strange about the black ones."

Then they hurried up the hill and disappeared toward the house.

As soon as they were out of sight, I stepped outside and sat on the stoop. Dragonflies buzzed over the cattails. A gassy smell wafted in over the marsh water. My head was reeling and my chest was heavy as a millstone. How had I ended up way out here in the middle of this swamp, trapped with these creepy aunts who I'd never even heard of until now?

No matter what Serena said, I knew what had really happened. I'd been wrapped up in some kind of bizarre, bone-crushing cocoon and nearly suffocated to death.

I hugged my knees up close to my chest, tight as I could. On top of being scared half out of my wits, I was mad.

Boiling mad. How could Mama and Poppers have gone off like that? How could they run off and leave me with a couple of aunts that Mama hadn't even spoken to in fifteen years? Or was there something else going on that no one was telling me?

As mad as I was, I wished more than anything that I was back home with my folks and everything was returned to normal. We'd all be sitting down to breakfast about now. It was Monday, the day Poppers always made his world-famous apple fritters. Mama would be reading us Mottie Klopp's Society Chatter from the *Cold Creek Junction Herald*. Poppers would snort at the report of Beatrice Fump's latest trip down-country: Would her brother, the award-winning opera singer, come fetch her in his Cole Aero-Eight Sportster? Or would she go by first-class railcar? Dandy and Bloomers would be chewing sweet clover out in the meadow. I'd go swimming in the creek with Jeb and Cora Washburn. I could almost hear the bullfrogs croaking their hearts out down at Plinketts' pond. . . .

And that's when it hit me.

I could run away if I wanted to!

There was nothing really stopping me if I put my mind to it. All I had to do was follow the road back through the swamp. I could head for Blossom Springs when I got to the split. The whole trip couldn't be more than nine or ten miles. If I set off now, there'd be plenty of daylight. It would sure be better than another night with Serena and Agnes, sleeping out in a woodshed that was ready to topple into the marsh.

I stood up, jittery with excitement. The trick was just to up and do it. Don't think about it—*just go*.

My eye followed the road as it came down the hill from the house. My legs turned to noodles.

Just go.

I snatched up my carpetbag from inside and hurried toward the road, aiming for the place where it met up with the swamp. Then I stopped . . . my heart went to lead.

Impossible . . .

The road was completely overgrown by swamp oaks. Thousands and thousands of them—spindly black trees, their branches twisted together like groping fingers. They rocked back and forth, their scraggly leaves thrashing wildly, even though there was hardly any wind to speak of.

How could such a thing happen? How could trees sprout up overnight so thick that they covered the road?

The track showed through in places—enough so that my eye could follow it out into the swamp. Maybe there was still hope. All I had to do was keep the lane in sight and I'd be okay.

Maybe.

Slowly, I took a couple steps toward the marsh . . . then a couple more. All at once, the swamp oaks stopped swaying. Their leaves quivered and rattled, and an eerie hiss filled the air.

I ran all the way to my aunts' house without looking back.

I sat on my aunts' front porch for a long time, confused, shaken, and without the slightest notion of what to do next. I knew better than to go inside until I'd fetched the eggs. But I was afraid to move. Those hissing swamp oaks had spooked the nerve right out of me. There was no mention of such a tree in *Hodgeworth's Encyclopedia*, I was sure of it. I knew every tree in all of New England by name, leaf, and habitat.

It occurred to me that my aunts had to have some way of getting out through those swamp oaks—knowing Serena, she probably just plowed them down with the Franklin. If I could only talk them into driving me back to Dredmoore Hollow . . .

I decided I would make them a nice breakfast to put them in a good mood before I asked. It was a long shot. But if that didn't work, I'd be stuck in Moaning Marsh until my folks came to fetch me. It might be days. Or longer. So I stood up, gritted my teeth, and forced myself to get on with it.

You can usually find a chicken coop by following the cackles, but not with this bunch. They were ghostly quiet. They weren't much for laying, either. There must've been two dozen chickens in that henhouse and only ten eggs for the bunch. I left the three black eggs alone, like Serena had said, and I was happy to do it. I'd never heard of black eggs before. The rooster—a scruffy bantam with beady red eyes—watched me from a corner roost.

I piled the eggs into the front of my shirt and padded

them with hay to keep them from banging together. Then I hurried out of the henhouse, my mouth watering at the thought of fried eggs and bacon. Anxious as I was to get away from my aunts' place, I realized I hadn't had any sort of a meal since the morning before. I was dizzy with hunger.

No sooner had I ducked through the henhouse door than someone grabbed the back of my neck. I let out a scream and dropped the eggs. An enormous hand grabbed the back of my pants and hoisted me high off the ground. Whoever had ahold of me was as strong as a bear. I tried to kick and flail, but he tightened his grip and I went limp. His footsteps were thunderous, and there was a foul smell in the air like licorice.

There was something else, too. Something big and dark, loping along next to us—I couldn't move my head to get a clear look. It snarled and grunted as we pounded across the barnyard toward the house.

When we came to the back stoop, the brute carrying me aimed a heavy kick at the door. He thumped it a dozen times or so, growling and cursing under his breath, till finally the door swung open.

Serena stood in the doorway with a fierce look in her eyes. Then she saw me dangling there, gasping for help, and her expression turned to surprise.

"Mercy sakes, Mr. Grobbs!" she cried. "Put that boy down!"

The giant hand lowered me to the doorstep but kept a firm hold on the back of my neck.

"Caught him rooting around in the henhouse," said a

gravelly voice just behind my ear. The stink of licorice made me gag.

"Of course he was in the henhouse," said Serena. "He was fetching eggs for breakfast."

She pulled me loose of the man's grip and turned me around to face him. "Elijah, this is Mr. Grobbs, our hired man."

My legs almost gave out. I opened my mouth to scream, but stopped myself. My eyes went straight to the man's left arm. Instead of a hand, he had nothing but a stump wrapped in a dirty rag. And standing next to him was a great hunch-backed mountain of a wolf.

No question about it, these two were the pair I'd seen that night in the graveyard. The two that dug the hole under Phineas Dredmoore's statue. I'd never gotten a good look at the man's face on account of his hood, but everything else was dead on. He was short and broad as a tree trunk.

Serena said he was her hired hand?

The wolf raised his lip and snarled at me, showing a row of yellow fangs as long as my fingers.

"Mr. Grobbs," said Serena, "this is my nephew, Elijah Twisp. He'll be staying with us for a time while his mother and father tend to some family matters."

The man stared at me darkly. Most of his face was lost in beard. A wide-brimmed hat cast a shadow over his eyes, so that all I could see of his face was a broad, battered nose and sunburned cheeks. A twig of licorice root hung from his lips. His grimy barn coat hung open, and I could see half a dozen hand axes, all different sizes, hanging from his belt.

"I'll bet Elijah'd be a big help clearing those swamp oaks off the Marsh Road," Serena went on. "Once that's done, there's another batch of Magic Snippers coupons for you to take in to Blossom Springs."

Grobbs's silence put a frost in the air. He ran a finger along the blade of one of his hatchets.

"Oh, you two are going to get along wonderfully, I can already tell!" Serena glanced back and forth between the two of us, glowing. "Elijah, you'll be happy to know that Mr. Grobbs is an expert on the natural wonders of Moaning Marsh. Be sure to have him take you down to the sink holes and show you where the muskrats nest. Yes, indeed. You two are like peas in a pod. I'm never wrong about these things."

"You never said nothing about no boy," growled Grobbs.

Serena's face went red. "Now, Mr. Grobbs,"–she spoke extra slow–"you keep a good eye on my nephew, you hear? I'm counting on you."

She pulled a necklace from under her blouse. There was a tiny glass bottle hitched to the end like a locket. The bottle was full of green liquid. She gave it a shake and raised an eyebrow at him. Her fox wrap grinned toothily.

Grobbs sneered back at her. "Don't you worry, Mizz Dredmoore. I ain't forgot our bargain. Just didn't know that tending to brats was part of the job."

Serena tucked the bottle back under her blouse. "A hired man does whatever needs doing."

Grobbs spat a clump of licorice root, knocking a bee off

a yellow daylily. He gave me one last glare, then turned and plodded off toward the swamp.

The look in his eye was pure murder.

7

Roobeelus Roobarbus

I WAS SO RATTLED BY THE SIGHT OF GROBBS AND his hunchback wolf that I messed up my first three tries at making breakfast. I kept glancing out the window for fear they'd come back while my aunts weren't around. I burnt the biscuits and busted the egg yolks and splattered bacon grease all over the floor.

I tried to work out a plan for where I'd hide if those two showed up. But all the doors in the house were locked. The only rooms I could get into were the kitchen, the pantry, and the indoor water closet–which were the rooms that Agnes told me I'd be cleaning. Why in Sam Hill would my aunts lock up every door in the house? It was clear they weren't too happy about having me around–especially Agnes–so why had they brought me here at all?

After all that work I did fixing breakfast, my aunts never touched a bite. They were expecting customers at the Magic Snippers and that was all they could think about. They kept hauling boxes full of junk out to the beauty shop–I could hear bottles clinking and liquid sloshing every time they went by. I got the feeling they hadn't had many customers up to this point. Between the swamp-side location and Agnes's happy-go-lucky disposition, it wasn't hard to decipher why.

When they were headed out to the barn with their final load, Agnes stopped to give me a distrustful leer. "Soon as you've cleaned the kitchen, go straight out to the marsh and help Mr. Grobbs, you hear? And stay clear of the Magic Snippers–you've got no business near that barn."

"Oh, Sister!" said Serena with a chuckle. "I think our nephew is clever enough to know the beauty shop is no place for a young man. Isn't that so, Elijah?"

"Yes'm," I said, and it was the truth. I didn't want to be any-where near Agnes when she was holding a pair of scissors.

"If I had my druthers," said Serena, casting a longful glance out the window, "I'd be working outdoors, too, Elijah. Goodness me! I'd rather be out felling swamp oaks in the fresh air any old day."

"It's the ragweed that needs chopping," snapped Agnes. Her nose was red from allergies. She glared at me. "You tell Mr. Grobbs I said so."

"Why, I might even come out and join you one of these days, Elijah," said Serena, as if cutting weeds was the finest thing she could ever imagine. "Sister, you'll have to tend the shop without me one morning."

Agnes rolled her eyes, and clomped off toward the barn with her load of supplies.

"Oh," said Serena, snapping her fingers. "Don't let me forget. I mixed up a new remedy to take care of that rash on your chin. We'll fix you up before bed tonight. Think you can remind me?"

"Yes'm," I lied. I'd go skinny-dipping in Moaning Marsh at midnight before I'd let my aunts touch me with another one of their remedies. Besides, I'd checked myself over in the water closet mirror, and the worst I could see was a couple reddish spots–most likely from all my aunts' pinching and prodding.

Serena tousled my hair, then scurried off after her sister, humming to herself.

I had no intention of cutting swamp oaks, ragweed, or anything else with Grobbs. He'd made it plain as day how he felt about me. And with that hunchback wolf he had for a pet, I intended to keep a good safe distance.

While I was dragging out the kitchen chores as best I could, I came across something interesting mixed in with a stack of newspapers and circulars on top of the butcher's block. It was a coupon for the Magic Snippers. I'd heard Serena tell Grobbs to pass them around down in Blossom Springs:

CONGRATULATIONS!

You Have Been Selected

To Receive

ONE FREE BEAUTY TREATMENT

at

THE MAGIC SNIPPERS

Beauty Salon

⚜ Serena & Agnes Dredmoore ⚜
will turn your blemishes into beauty!
No problem is too big for our Special Beauty Remedies!
Our well-appointed salon is located just 9 short miles from
Blossom Springs at the end of scenic Moaning Marsh Road.

Open 9 AM to 4 PM Monday through Friday.
No Appointment Necessary.

It was a real professional-looking coupon with fancy doodles all around the edges. But why hadn't my aunts set up shop closer to town? Maybe that's why the first visit was free. Any place in the world would be better than Moaning Marsh.

After I'd swept, scrubbed, and polished everything in the kitchen, I went to the front door and peeked outside. There was no sign of Grobbs and his wolf. I knew they were supposed to be out in the marsh, clearing swamp oaks off the road, but that did little to comfort me.

I'd barely stepped out onto the porch when a Model T Runabout truck came rattling up over the hill and parked in front of the Magic Snippers. The sight of that truck sent a jolt of pure joy through every inch of my body.

Customers!

My aunts had customers!

It seemed impossible—but there they were. I didn't care who they were or where they'd come from. The fact that, sooner or later, they'd be headed back home meant one thing to me. . . .

I could hitch a ride out of Moaning Marsh.

I could escape!

Three teenage girls tumbled out of the Runabout, giggling and jostling each other. Their voices were so loud that Grobbs's wolf set to howling somewhere off in the marsh. The laughter slowly petered out as the girls took in the picture: the rundown farmhouse, the dead trees and scraggly witchgrass, the Magic Snippers sign hanging cockeyed on the side of the barn.

The shortest of the three–a stout, bug-eyed gal–was clearly having second thoughts about this adventure. She tried to pull the driver back into the truck. But the girl shook her off, laughing and swatting at her with an enormous yellow hat covered in plastic fruits and canaries. The third gal was bigger than the other two put together. She tottered up to the Snippers' door, clutching a swollen red purse against her chest.

Serena swooped out of the shop, all smiley and welcoming. I couldn't make out what she was saying–but she fawned over the bunch of them something sickening, fussing over their hair and outfits. Before the girls knew what was happening, Serena herded all three of them inside. Seconds later, a CLOSED sign appeared in the Snippers' front window and the shades dropped.

Very strange.

I watched the door, desperately pondering the situation. First of all, what was going on in there that would prompt my aunts to close up shop? And more importantly: how could I hitch a ride from these gals without getting caught?

There was a big patch of ragweed a few steps away from the girls' Runabout. I noticed that Grobbs had left a scythe, a rake, and a mess of other tools poking out of a wheelbarrow next to the barn. Perfect! I ran for the wheelbarrow and wheeled it up close to the girls' truck. Then I went to work cutting ragweed.

Or, at least, I pretended to.

While I was chopping away, another motor sounded from across the marsh. When it rains, it pours! I could hardly believe my luck.

A shiny white car rumbled up over the hill, and didn't my heart take a joyful bound. It was one of the new Packards–a Single-Eight. I'd seen pictures in Mama's *House & Garden* magazine, but I'd never seen one close up. It was a beauty.

The driver hopped out of the car and dusted off his sports coat and trousers, both of which were spotless white, same as the Packard. He was a round-faced little man with a spindly mustache. His hair was slicked back with so much grease, it looked like he'd just got out of the bathtub. The Packard was crammed full of boxes, crates, and cages.

"You must be the nephew!" he said the minute he caught sight of me. He hurried toward me, glancing around nervously.

He reached to shake my hand, and I noticed he was wearing driving gloves–black leather ones like I'd seen in race-car magazines.

"My name's Japeth Dredmoore," he said. "I do believe

we're kin, you and I. Second cousins once removed and up a step, or thereabouts."

"My name's Elijah," I said.

An alarm went off in my head. I was pretty sure I'd heard his name before—didn't he have something to do with the Lullabeetle Silk?

A muffled squawk came from one of the crates in the Packard. The noise set off a bunch of scuffling and scratching throughout the pile. There were strange words scrawled on the sides of the boxes:

Croneswort
Mimicker's Quills
Midnight Moon-Blood
Corpseweed Root
Welsh Goat Whiskers

"Do tell me, Nephew," he said, moving closer than I liked. "Are you having an enjoyable visitation with my dear cousin Serena?"

He seemed to be staring at my chin.

"Yessir," I said. "It's all right, I guess."

"Good, good . . ." he said, absently. His eyes were still locked on to my jaw. "It's a fine thing for a youthful feller, such as yourself, to venture forth and embracify new experiences—*veni, vidi, voochi,* as they say in Latinia. Let me guess, now . . . you must be . . . oh, goodness, about twelve years old?"

"Er . . . eleven, sir. Twelve next October."

"Please," he said, "call me Japeth. None of this *sir* business. We're kin, after all!"

"That's a swell-looking Packard," I said, stepping toward the car and away from his stare. "I read in a magazine that those Single-Eights have special four-tire brakes and a built-in chassis lubricator."

"You don't say?" He stole a look toward the Magic Snippers.

"It sure would be keen to get a peek at that motor," I said.

He let out a shriek. "Goodness, me oh my!"

At first, I thought he was peeved that I touched his car, but then he craned in close to my chin. His hair smelled like perfume.

"That's a frightful rash you've got coming in on your *chompular jaw-flabbulus*!" he croaked.

I reached up to feel my chin, but he grabbed my hand. Had my aunts been right about the swamp rash?

"Whatever you do, don't touch it!" His eyes were serious. "That's a full-on Roobeelus Roobarbus infection. If you scratch it, it'll spread like wildfire."

He shook his head and clicked his tongue.

"So far it's only got hold of your *lower whiskernius* region, which is merely a superfractional condition. But if you don't tend to it immediately, it could easily multicate into a rarified deadly fungus known as Blithering Brain Rot."

"Blithering Brain Rot?" I started to laugh, figuring he was pulling my leg. But Japeth never cracked a smile.

"Is your eyesight going blurry?" He wagged a finger back and forth in front of my eyes.

"I don't think so," I said.

"Funny taste in your mouth?" He smacked his lips. "Like boot polish or spoiled pumpkins?"

I shook my head. The more he went on about it, the more I longed to reach up and feel my chin.

"Well, there's no point in taking chances." He took my arm and walked me around to the back of the Packard.

"It was Roobeelus Roobarbus that killed poor Uncle Ichabod over in Moppshire, Scotland," he went on. "What a horrifical way to go! The fungus spread slowly through his brain till his *orba peeperus*—which is to say his eyeballs—detachified completely from his head. A week later his teeth and tongue came loose. Then, finally, his entire *crania skullimus* caved in. His brain had been completely consumicated by Roobeelus fungus!"

He stared at me in horror. I didn't know what to say. It was like something out of those *Strange But True* magazines they sold down at the dry goods store—between all his ridiculous words and the story about Uncle Ichabod's caved-in brain. But why was he saying these things? He sure didn't act like he was joking.

"Lucky for you," said Japeth, "I just happen to have a first-rate brain rot remedy in the back of my automobile!" He snuck another glance at the beauty shop, then started digging through the boxes.

"Actually," I said, edging away from the Packard,

"I feel just fine. Honest."

He grabbed hold of me and shoved me up against the car. None too gently, either.

"Nonsense," he said with a chill in his voice. "No cousin of mine is going to have his brain rotticated by some vicious fungus! No sir, indeed!"

He held on to my suspenders with one hand and continued to dig through the crates with the other. Squeals and snarls came from the boxes as they toppled over.

"Ah!" he shouted. "Here it is! Roobeelus Roobarbus Remedy!"

He held up a blue bottle.

"You haven't touched any dead cats today, have you?" he asked.

"Please, Cousin Japeth . . ." I struggled to pull loose. "I really don't want–"

"It's absolutely harmless!" he said. "And mmm-mmm! A delectulous blueberry flavor!"

He pulled the stopper out of the bottle, and a vinegar stink filled the air. "Now, just tip your head back and–"

"Cousin Japeth!" Serena's voice rang from across the yard.

Japeth fumbled the bottle. He spilt blue goop all over his sleeve as he slipped the bottle, still open, into his pocket. Then he spun around with his arms spread wide.

"Dearest Cousin Serena!"

She pitched toward us, looking back and forth between me and Japeth, her eyes dark with suspicion. I'd have sworn her fox wrap let out a snarl.

"I didn't hear you pull up," she said. "Looks like you met my nephew already."

"Ah, yes. We're old kinsmen now, aren't we, Elias?" He slapped me on the back.

He bent over in a swoony sort of bow as he hurried up to her. He went to kiss her hand, but she pulled away. Unfazed, he tittered and kissed her knee instead.

"Oh, Serena dearest! Come see what I brought you!" He sprang toward the Packard, fanning his arm across all the crates and cages. "Our friends overseas were most accommodatious with the sundries you asked for. They managed to procurify even the rarest and most potent items!"

She studied the jumble, reading the words on each crate as if they spelled out the meaning of life. She seemed to forget that Japeth and I were standing there. Then, suddenly, she spun back around, fluttering her eyelashes.

"Wonderful! Absolutely wonderful!" She gave Japeth a little pat on the arm. His knees buckled and he giggled.

"Exactly what the Snippers needed!" she said.

"Right, right!" clucked Japeth, winking and tugging on his earlobe. He threw a glance at me. "Just the usual ol' stock and trade beauty supplies! Hair tonics . . . skin smoothifiers . . . *les parfumes des toilets* . . . all the necessities of beautification!"

Serena's face turned serious. "You didn't help prepare any of the supplies, did you?"

Japeth threw his hands up. "No, dearest cousin! Of course not! I would never–"

"Not Silas or Seth, either?"

"My beloved Serena!" cried Japeth, stumbling backward as if he'd been shot square in the heart. "Surely, truly, you must know I always follow your instructions to the most explicit and exactifica–"

She put a finger to his lips. "Of course . . . of course you do, Cousin Japeth!"

His ears blushed the color of raspberries.

"Well, now, Elijah." She put her hand on my shoulder and guided me away from the Packard. "I'm sure all this beauty shop business is boring you witless. Why don't you run off and find Mr. Grobbs? The two of you can finish chopping that ragweed for your poor sniffly Auntie Agnes? Hmm?"

I looked over at Japeth. He'd made no mention of Blithering Brain Rot in front of Serena. He tugged anxiously at the ends of his mustache and gazed off at the clouds.

So, I started across the grass toward the wheelbarrow. A minute later, I saw the two of them heading toward the Magic Snippers, Cousin Japeth bent low beneath a heap of crates and boxes.

8

Piscatory Pox

IT MUST'VE BEEN AFTER MIDNIGHT BY THE TIME
Japeth drove off across Moaning Marsh. Orange moonlight
shimmered like fire on the roof of his Packard. The three
girls stayed at the Magic Snippers the whole night. I kept
watch through a knothole in the wall next to my cot. The
Model T Runabout never budged from its parking spot.
They were supposed to be my escape plan, and I was determined not to let them slip off without me.

One thing was clear enough: this was no normal beauty
treatment those gals were getting. Lights flashed in the barn
windows, and green smoke slithered into the air through
the cupola. There was crazy laughter. Explosions rattled the
walls. Something or some*body* jumped out of the Dutch
doors from the top floor of the barn—it looked like they were
trying to fly.

No one came to lock the door of the guest cottage (by
which I mean *woodshed*) that night. Nor did anyone call

for me in the morning. As far as I could tell, my aunts spent the whole day locked up inside the Snippers with those three girls.

It was late afternoon when Agnes finally showed her face, and I didn't need to be a mind reader to see she was in a temper. As soon as she saw me, her nostrils flared and her eyes went to slits.

"What are you doing, hiding away in the kitchen when there's ragweed that needs chopping?"

"I . . . I made breakfast for you and Aunt Serena," I stammered. "But nobody showed up."

"Breakfast?" She snorted. "You think we have time for breakfast? With those dimwit girls out there, and everything coming out a fouled-up mess? This is all thanks to your high-and-mighty mother! If Sister just listened to me, we'd already have—"

She stopped, and her eyes lit up greedily. She stared at me, pondering in silence for a moment.

"You wait right here!" she said at last. Then she disappeared behind one of the locked doors down the hallway.

A gramophone inside my head blasted out a warning—
RUN!
RUN NOW!
Naturally, I froze in place.

In no time she was back, a bundle of black cloth in her hand, her purple eyes blazing madly. She snagged her parasol under my arm and dragged me to the water closet.

"Sister's been too gentle with you!" she hissed. "We

should've strapped you down to the cot like I said. That Lullabeetle Silk would've done its job, and we'd have what we need by now. Most likely, you'd have smothered to death, but that's no concern of mine."

She aimed a sneer in the direction of the Magic Snippers. "Well, *she* won't stop me this time. If she thinks those three girls are going to be any help, she's got a hole in her brain! I'm not waiting . . . not anymore . . . not when there's *other* ways. . . ."

"Please, Aunt Agnes," I pleaded. "I didn't mean to—"

"Quiet, boy!" she snapped, sending a tremor through her towering hair. "Fifteen years I been biding my time, thanks to your mama and her superior ways. She may as well have cut off my hands and feet!"

She unwrapped the bundle of black rags and stole a nervous glance out the water-closet door. A cold, sick feeling spilled over me. I backed into the table, knocking the pitcher over. It shattered in the washbasin.

"This'll go on for years if we do it her way," Agnes muttered under her breath. "Why should Serena always get the say? I'll show her a thing or two. Then we'll see who's in charge!"

She took a crooked willow stick and a small tin from the clump of rags. There was a dried-up fishtail tied to one end of the stick. The tin was scrawled with the words

Hornpout Powder

"Hold still, boy!" She came at me with a long strip of cloth.

I tried to duck away, but she grabbed hold of my ear and

pinned me against the wall. She was amazingly strong. She wrapped one arm around me, clamping both my hands to my sides.

"It'll only be worse if you squirm!" She wrapped the rag around my face, starting just above my mouth. 'Round and 'round she went, tight as she could. She wrapped over my eyes and all the way up my forehead. Only my mouth and chin showed through. I was completely blinded. That night of the Lullabeetle Silk came flashing back.

"Please!" I cried. "I'll be good—"

"Don't you move, boy!" she snarled into my ear. "It'll all be over in a flash."

My mouth went dry as sawdust.

There was a squeaking sound—she was opening the tin of Hornpout Powder. A foul, fishy smell filled the air. My mind raced, searching for a plan. Her fingers jabbed my chin as she dabbed on the powder. The stink was unbearable.

"There we go!" she snickered. Her breath was hot on my neck. "Right on the tip of the chin . . . that's right . . . good and thick . . . oh, that's perfect."

I felt the prickly ends of the willow stick poking at my jaw . . . and something inside of me snapped.

The blindfold.

The monstrous stink of the Hornpout Powder.

Agnes's claw-fingered grip.

The fright of it all rushed over me, and I let out such a scream that it made my own ears ring. My arms shot up, breaking free of her stranglehold. My hand bumped the willow stick, and I grabbed it . . . wrapped my fingers tight . . . wrestled against her grasp . . . both of us shouting, thrashing, struggling . . .

An explosion went off.

The stick blasted to pieces in my hand. The force of the blast hurled me backward into the bathtub. I heard Agnes crash, shrieking, into the door. The Hornpout tin clattered across the floor.

I tore the blindfold off my eyes as Agnes struggled to her feet. Her face was covered in green powder.

She clawed at her cheeks with both hands. "What have you done to me? You ruined it! *You ruined it!*"

She sprang for the washbasin and splashed water over her face in a wild fury. I scrambled out of the bathtub, ready to make a run for it, just as Serena burst into the room.

"What happened? I heard screaming!" She held a stick in one hand, raised up like she was ready to switch somebody.

Grobbs charged into the doorway behind her with a hatchet at the ready.

They both stood there a minute, dead silent, and took in the scene. Serena's stick disappeared under her fox wrap. Grobbs lowered the ax to his shoulder, and a dark grin stole over his face.

"What have you done?" I didn't know whether Serena was talking to me or her sister. Her eyes went straight to my chin.

In all that commotion, I'd forgotten that Agnes had covered my jaw with stinky fish powder. I snatched up a rag and scrubbed as hard as I could.

"What did you put on the boy's face?" Serena's eyes were a thunderstorm. Grobbs let out a raspy chuckle and tromped off down the hall.

Agnes turned to face her sister. "Your plan was taking too long! The boy couldn't be trusted. So I decided to do it my way and–"

"What did you put on his face?" hollered Serena.

Agnes cringed behind her parasol.

"Hornpout Powder!" she shouted back. "I did just like it says in all the books. But the boy grabbed hold of the stick–"

Agnes went silent, her mouth locked open, a look of horror in her eyes. Her face took on a strange glow. She reached up and felt her cheeks and nose. They began to swell and ripple, pulsing like a bullfrog's throat. She howled in fright.

"My face! What's happening?"

"You *touched* the powder!" shouted Serena. "How could you be so stupid?"

My own skin started to tingle. I reached up to my chin, and my heart stopped cold. I could feel blisters puffing and throbbing, just like Agnes's. A dim green glow rose from my skin.

"You fool!" Serena grabbed Agnes by the hair and pushed her face up close to my jaw. "Look what you've done to him!"

She took hold of Agnes's wrist and held up her hand. Her fingers were swelled up and glowing.

My jaw throbbed like it was going to explode.

"What's happening to me?" I said with a whimper. My knees went weak, and I fell back against the wall.

"Piscatory Pox!" yelled Serena. She grabbed her sister around the throat and squeezed. "You gave the boy Piscatory Pox!"

Agnes's ears turned red as Serena throttled her. Agnes clawed at her sister's hands and gasped for air. The skin on her face began to go crusty. Scales appeared. Ruddy green ones, like the skin of some grotesque fish.

My hands trembled as I ran my fingers over my chin–my skin was going coarse and scaly, too.

Serena let go, and Agnes dropped to the floor.

"I'm disfigured!" moaned Agnes. "I'm hideous!"

She pawed at her face so desperately that I almost felt sad for her.

"You deserve worse," hissed Serena. "It'll be a week before those scales come off the boy's face."

"A . . . a . . . week?" gasped Agnes. "We can't wait a week!"

"That's right, Sister," said Serena. "If you'd left the boy alone and done as I said, the girls would be ready, and we'd get what we needed in a day or two. Now it'll be a week, maybe longer."

It was a relief to hear that at least the scales weren't permanent.

"How could I have known–" Agnes started. Serena cut her off.

"How could you have known?" she spat. I inched my way back into a corner, my chin throbbing, my skin on fire with itch. "Because everything you do turns out this way. It always has and always will. Every time we get a new bunch of girls up here, something goes wrong on account of your impatient, reckless–"

"None of those were my fault!" shrieked Agnes, still sprawled on the floor. "It's the curse that ruined–"

"You dropped a *glove* in the Crone Spittle Tonic! A *glove*!"

I had no idea what they were talking about. My skin burned so bad I wanted to die.

"You're the one who got us in this bind," said Serena, her voice quiet now, but sharp as glass. "You and your headstrong stupidity. All these years and you haven't learned a thing."

Agnes stared up from the floor, red faced and shaking. I could feel the hatred coming off her like heat.

Serena stepped toward the door as if she was about to leave. Then she stopped and turned to her sister with a glare that chilled me to the bone.

"I would've been the one, you know. I would've been chosen. You took that from me once, Sister dear. I'm not about to let you ruin it again. From now on you do exactly as I say. And leave the boy to me."

9

Strangle Oaks

THAT NIGHT, I LAY ON MY COT, ITCHY AND sleepless. My fingers kept sneaking up to my face to feel the Piscatory Pox. What kind of poison was in that Hornpout Powder that would make a person break out in fish scales? Serena had said the scales should go away in a week or so, but it was hard not to worry. And why were they so infernally fixed on my chin, anyway? What had Agnes intended that powder to do?

Anything could happen in this horrible nightmare place. *Anything.*

I heard a motor start up. I peered out of the knothole next to my bed just as the Runabout lurched from its parking spot and sputtered across the barnyard. I groaned in despair. My aunts' customers were finally headed home. Without me. Agnes had locked the shed door, spoiling my plan to sneak a ride in the girls' truck. Two days they'd been hidden away in the Magic Snippers. What sort of beauty treatment took two whole days? What if no one else came? How was I going to get out of here?

The wind whistled through the swamp oaks. It battered the window boards and rattled the door on its hinges. I wanted to bust my way out of the shed and run as far away as I could . . . away from my aunts and Grobbs and Moaning Marsh. I wanted to, but I was too much of a coward . . . especially at night with the wind out there howling like a hungry wolf, and swamp oaks sprouting up all over the road.

If only Mama and Poppers knew what was happening to me—how I wished they'd hurry up and come. I couldn't help but feel a bit angry at Grandma Ester, too. It was her fault that I'd ended up here—why couldn't she keep her balloon on the ground like a normal grandmother?

Of course, that only got me to worrying about her, wherever she was. And then I felt awful for getting mad in the first place. There was no knowing what had gone wrong. I couldn't count on anything my aunts had told me.

I tried to take my mind off my misery by reading about Tom Swift's fearless search for the sunken steamship the SS *Pandora*. There's nothing to distract a fellow from his worries like a Tom Swift adventure. He was afraid of nothing, that Tom. There was no machine he couldn't build, no danger he couldn't work his way out of. If he'd been stuck in my predicament, he would've rigged the woodshed up with airplane wings and a motor, and he'd have flown right out of that swamp.

But me? I wedged the door shut with three hunks of kindling, no matter it was already locked and bolted. Then I wrapped the blankets tight around my ears to block out the croaks and groans echoing off the marsh.

I woke to the sound of boots on the front stoop. I sat up in a daze as the door banged open and Grobbs's mountainous shape filled the doorway. Morning light streamed into the shed, along with the bitter stink of licorice root. The hunchback wolf stood at Grobbs's side, ready to leap, drool dripping from his yellow fangs.

"Stay, Jack!"

The wolf froze in place, his eyes fixed on my Adam's apple.

"It's time you and me had a talk." Grobbs glanced back toward the house.

His eyes went to the green scales on my face and his eyebrows furrowed. He went quiet for a minute, then spat a mouthful of licorice root out the door.

"See, truth is," he said, "I ain't so keen on having a boy underfoot. 'Specially not a Dredmoore boy."

"N-n-no, sir . . . I'll just keep to the woodshed if you want." I considered explaining that I was actually a *Twisp*, but he didn't seem in the mood for particulars.

He pushed up the edge of his hat with his stump arm. He held an ax in his good hand–he used the blade to scratch his ear.

"Dangerous place for a boy, Moaning Marsh." He grinned, baring a set of crooked teeth, black with licorice juice. "If the bog holes don't get you, the Strangle Oaks will."

He took a step closer, and the stench of licorice hit me full on.

"On the other hand . . ." He lowered his voice to a deep whisper. "Me and Jack clear the Strangle Oaks off that road every mornin', Sisters' orders. Fast growers, them oaks. I cut 'em down every mornin' and they spring right back every night, even meaner than before. Unnatural, I'd call it."

"Yessir," I said.

"Now, if a boy was to set out across the marsh one mornin', once them Strangle Oaks was cut off the road, and if he kept up a steady hoof and stuck to the track . . . why, I bet he'd make Blossom Springs in four or five hours. Even a scrawny, no-account Dredmoore boy."

I nodded anxiously.

Was my aunts' hired man telling me to run away? Or was this some kind of trick?

He turned and looked out across the swamp. An endless army of spindly trees–Strangle Oaks, he'd called them– swayed back and forth, branches entwined. Grobbs spat out a gob of licorice root.

"C'mon, Jack!" he called. The wolf wrenched his eyes away from my throat and sprang to his master's side.

"Keep an eye on those oaks," Grobbs growled back over his shoulder. "Soon as you see that road's clear, you best find your way out of here . . . *while you still can.*"

He waded into the bog, whistling. As he raised his ax, a shudder ran through the Strangle Oaks, and a frightful hissing sound filled the air.

10

Tassles & Toads

GRANDMA ESTER ONCE TOLD ME THAT IT'S loathsome bad luck to cross paths with a one-armed man. She didn't know the half of it. My one-armed man had a hatchet and a hunchback wolf.

Had he really meant what he said about running away?

Maybe it was a trap. But if he really had it in for me, he could easily snatch me out of the woodshed any time he pleased.

I hurried up to the house to do the morning chores, my heart thumping away like a drum. I turned the situation over in my mind: I could tell my aunts about Grobbs. . . . If they knew he tried to scare me into running away, maybe they'd fire him. At least, that would be one problem out of the way–then I'd only need to figure a way out of Moaning Marsh.

But if I ratted and they didn't do anything . . . then I'd be in double deep. There was some sort of deal between the three of them—something to do with that bottle Serena kept on a necklace.

And then there was Grobbs's warning . . . *find your way out of here while you still can.*

I was about to reach for the doorknob when I spied the black tower of Agnes's hair rising up in the kitchen window, which was propped open with a moonshine jug. Agnes had her back to me—she was peering into a mirror, moaning in misery.

That open window put an idea in my head.

My feet went into action before my brain had a chance to ask questions. Next thing I knew, I was squatting in a patch of yellow daylilies right under the windowsill.

"It's not working!" Agnes whined. "The scales are still showing through!"

"Here, let me," said Serena. "You didn't put it on thick enough."

By the sound of it, they were trying to cover up Agnes's Piscatory Pox with one of their concoctions.

"Still too lumpy!" said Agnes. "And now my cheeks are all pink."

"Looks better than fish scales," said Serena. "You're lucky you came out of it as good as you did, Sister. If it wasn't for the curse muddling things up, you'd be splashing around in the swamp right now with catfish whiskers and a tail."

"The book never warned about a moon on the wane!" snapped Agnes.

"Moon or no moon," said Serena in a haughty tone, "you

had no business trying to potion the boy without me."

"I told you before . . . I was only trying to move things along faster," said Agnes. "If we'd just strapped him down from the start—"

"Now, Sister. We've been over this. These things take cleverness and patience, which nature saw fit to deny you. You need to let me make the decisions, so you can tend to the things you're good at."

There was a long, cold silence.

"And what exactly is it you think I'm good at?" Agnes's voice quavered with bitterness.

"Well . . . you know . . ." said Serena. "Other things."

"I've got the Dredmoore gift, same as you!" Agnes burst out.

"Of course you do. Now, let's not quarrel. Look . . . it's making your Piscatory Pox swell up."

Agnes let out a gasp.

By this time, the sensible part of my brain was screaming for me to get out from under that window before I got caught. But curiosity got the better of me—what was this *curse* they were talking about? And what did they mean by *Dredmoore gift*?

"We made good progress with those three Blossom Springs girls," Serena said in a cheery voice. "They're taking to the treatment even better than I expected."

"Taking too long if you ask me." Agnes snorted.

"The Croneswort Tonic that Cousin Japeth got from overseas will do wonders. You'll see. They'll be ready to do everything we need in a couple more visits."

"What makes you so sure they'll come back?" asked Agnes. "We should've locked them up in the shop like I wanted."

"Don't you worry about our new girls," said Serena with a chuckle. "I took precautions . . . as I always do. They'll fetch everything on the list and be back tomorrow morning, ready to do as they're told. We've just got to keep a close eye on that boy until his pox clear up."

"Speaking of the boy . . ." said Agnes. I heard her voice move closer to the window. "Shouldn't he be up here tending to breakfast by now?"

"Hmm," said Serena. "I sent Grobbs to get him ages ago."

Footsteps clattered across the kitchen floor. A second before the back door swung open, I dropped to my belly in the daylilies.

"BOOOOOOOOOOOY!" Agnes's voice echoed across the marsh.

I held my breath and lay as still as I could. An enormous bug crawled up my neck, and something prickly poked inside my ear. I clenched my teeth until the bug finally flew off. Agnes hollered a few more times, then went back inside, stomping and fuming.

"Calm down, Sister," said Serena. "You'll catch a lot more flies with honey. Only a few more days, and everything will be ready. Let the boy be until then."

One of them yanked the jug out from under the window, and it slammed shut with a startling *bang!*

The Witches of Dredmoore Hollow

Only a few more days?
What exactly would they do *then?*

The rest of the day, I kept a close eye on the Magic Snippers, hoping more customers would show up, but they never did. My carpetbag was packed and hidden in a patch of ferns, ready to go at a moment's notice. Agnes must've taken Serena's speech to heart, because she left me alone the whole day. To tell the truth, it was sort of unnerving. Nobody called for me at all. I could almost hear the sound of the clock tick-tick-ticking down the time as they waited for whatever it was they were waiting for.

My aunts were up to something dark and devious, that much I knew. Serena and Agnes were nothing like they first appeared—nothing like the sweet-talking, fancy-dressed gals who showed up unannounced back in Dredmoore Hollow. The things that went on around their place were worse than strange.

Lullabeetle Silk.
Strangle Oaks.
Piscatory Pox.
Who could even guess what went on inside the Magic Snippers?

But a suspicion had been growing in my head since the first night I'd come to Moaning Marsh, and now, after everything I'd seen and heard, I couldn't see any other explanation . . .

My aunts were witches.

I knew it was crazy to think such things. Poppers would've boxed my ears and told me to quit reading so many storybooks. But what other explanation was there? The very thought of it made me feel queasy and ridiculous all at once. There was no such thing as witches—everybody knew that.

But what if everybody was *wrong*?

The next day, I was up and ready to go by dawn. If Serena was right, those three gals with the Model T Runabout would be coming back, and this time I was going to be ready. I put my aunts' breakfast out on the table and went to work chopping weeds a short distance from the Snippers' front door.

I'd hardly got started when the girls' Runabout came rumbling up over the hill. I got so excited that I stabbed my leg with the pruning shears. I danced around in a circle for a minute, trying to remember where I'd stashed my carpetbag. Then I gave up on it altogether and ran toward the truck.

First thing I noticed was the gal sitting in the pickup bed. She'd been large last time I saw her, but this time, she was huge. *Like a giant.* She wore a flowery pink dress, big as a tent, and her head was festooned with a bouncing heap of pink and red ribbons. When she hoisted herself out of the truck bed, the back end lifted up about a foot.

The other two girls stepped out and shook the wrinkles from their dresses. I watched from behind the dead butternut tree, trying to decide which one to approach. While I was studying them over, a small figure slipped out of the pickup box and plunged into a thistle patch on the other side of the truck. The figure moved so fast that all I saw was a pair of clodhopper boots disappearing into the bushes.

The three girls didn't seem to notice.

I was fairly worked up. . . . Maybe I'd imagined it. . . .

The driver seemed taller and more twiggy than I remembered. Her eyes had gotten bigger—pretty but strange. Shimmery blue and glassy as marbles, with long, fluttering lashes. Her rosy cheeks seemed to be fixed in a permanent blush, and her too-red lips were locked in a demented smile. She was wearing one of those flapper dresses with bead tassels hanging off everywhere and the same yellow hat smothered in plastic fruits and canaries. The hat started to rise up off her head as if it was trying to float away. She grabbed hold of it and pinned it down.

The third gal was about the same size as before—short and well fed—but this time her hair was slicked tight against her face. A coat of blue lipstick shimmered on her lips. The same color circled her eyes, which bulged from her head, giving her the look of a startled toad. She paused before shutting the truck door, and a cascade of squirming shapes tumbled out onto the ground. It took me a moment to realize what they were: *toads*. Live, wriggling, warty-skinned toads. They gathered around her feet in a bouncing swarm.

I stood clinging to the butternut tree, paralyzed.

Had my aunts done this to them?

If they spent another day in the Magic Snippers, who knew how much worse they'd get?

The one in the flapper dress grabbed her hat again as it tried to fly off–this time she tied a bow under her chin. The group started toward the Snippers' door.

It was now or never. Odd as those gals looked, they were my best chance of escape.

"Hey there!" I called, racing after them. "Hold up a minute!"

All three stopped and turned with dazed expressions. Their hands hung limp at their sides. The giant one hummed to herself, tunelessly–a trickle of drool dribbled from the corner of her mouth. A couple of toads spilled out of the short one's purse and joined the others, swarming and pouncing around her ankles.

I stopped a few paces away, suddenly uncertain about my plan.

"I wouldn't go in there if I was you," I said, my voice cracking.

They stared at me, eyes glazed over.

"My aunts . . . they're . . . they're up to something bad."

The giant one stuck a finger up her nose and dug intently, still humming her tuneless song.

"You should get out of here while you can." I was feeling more desperate by the second. "Before they do something . . . something worse to you . . ."

The one in the canary hat let out a hiccup. The short, toad-faced gal yawned. All three of them turned lazily, and continued toward the door.

"Please!" I hollered. "You've got to believe me! You're in horrible danger!"

The toad-faced girl reached for the doorknob.

Without thinking, I sprang toward her and grabbed hold of her arm. She spun around so fast it didn't seem possible, her eyes blazing. She let out a beastly snarl. I stumbled away from her, flailing and gasping, as an army of squealing toads hurled themselves at my legs.

I choked back a scream, swatting wildly at the toads. All three girls moved toward me, nostrils flaring, a crazy look in their eyes–the short one smacked her lips and belched.

Whether they chased after me, I couldn't say. I ran without looking back. When I got to the woodshed, I jammed the door shut with a crate full of split alder wood.

11

Howling Moonbeast

THE SAME THREE GALS—IF THAT'S WHAT YOU could call them—came back the next day, and the day after that. I watched from a good, safe distance as they unloaded sacks full of God knows what from the back of their truck and tottered into the Magic Snippers, trailed by a writhing mob of toads.

The first time I'd seen those girls, they were a regular bunch of teenagers—sort of giggly and awkward, but no different from any other gals I knew. Now, after a few days at the Snippers, they lumbered around in silly outfits, grunting and snorting at each other, acting like their brains had short-circuited. Not to mention the *size* of the giant one. And the toads. And the flying hat.

I'd overheard Agnes and Serena through the window that day, talking about how well the girls were *taking to the treatment* . . . and how they'd be *ready* after a few more visits. Ready to do *what*? I had no idea. Whatever they were doing to the Blossom Springs girls seemed to tie into their plans for me. They needed all of us for something. But none of it made any sense.

Agnes and Serena didn't know about my run-in with their girls, or if they did, they never let on. They went along, same as always, Serena flashing her phony smiles, tousling my hair, and telling me my folks would come any day now–probably tomorrow. And Agnes kept her distance for the most part, scowling at me from afar like I was a bug she intended to squish when the time was right.

Serena had her foul moments, too. A dark cloud descended whenever she stopped to check my Piscatory Pox. She tried to hide her irritation behind a twitchy smile, but I saw the way she glared at Agnes, whose pox had turned to crusty scabs, just like mine.

We were waiting, all three of us, for the scabs to heal and the girls to be *ready*. What came after that . . . I was pretty darn certain that it wouldn't be good.

And now, my only plan for escape was ruined–I'd sooner play fetch with Grobbs's wolf than hitch a ride with those three deranged girls.

There had to be a better way out.

The Strangle Oaks' hissing chorus rose off the marsh, day and night, as if they were laughing at me.

After a whole week at my aunts' place without so much as a postcard from Mama and Poppers, I began to doubt they'd ever come. I wondered if they even knew where I was.

Every night, I took my jackknife and carved a mark into the wall next to my cot to track the passing days. It was sad and lonesome out in that woodshed at night. All I had to bide my time were a few Tom Swift books that I'd already read half a million times and a crystal radio that couldn't even pick up any signals. I missed my room and my big feather bed. I missed my books and my garden, fishing down at the Plinketts' pond, and swimming in Six-Mile Brook. I tried to tell myself it was only for a little while longer.

Serena noticed me moping and said she'd have Grobbs send a telegram up to Great Uncle Ezra's in hope that they'd found Grandma Ester. I didn't figure Serena would really send the note, but a couple days later I heard Agnes holler from the kitchen window:

"Boy! There's a letter from your folks! Get up here and read it before I toss it in the cookstove!"

I charged up to the house as fast as a jackrabbit, my heart racing with excitement. I knew better than to trust my aunts—but I couldn't keep myself from hoping.

Agnes tossed the letter on the floor and tromped out of the room.

My fingers trembled as I studied the envelope. It was still sealed, and if it was a fake, they'd sure done a good job. The postmark was from Klakkinook Bay, Northwest Territories, Canada. I headed for the kitchen table, thinking I'd better sit down. But just at that moment, I looked out the window and saw Grobbs trudging up the hill with a pitchfork over his shoulder and the wolf at his heels.

I dropped to my knees so I could peek out over the windowsill without being seen. If Grobbs came to the back stoop, I planned to make a run for the front door. I tucked the letter into my pocket.

As Grobbs came closer, I could see something wasn't right. He looked fidgety and anxious; his face was ghost white. Then I noticed the wolf: the creature limped and stumbled like he was about to keel over, tongue hanging out and muzzle nearly dragging on the ground.

Grobbs was only a few steps from the back door, and I was a hair-trigger from bolting, when Serena's voice rang across the lawn.

"Are you looking for me, Mr. Grobbs?"

Grobbs reached down and scratched his wolf's ears. "New moon tonight, Mizz Dredmoore."

She stepped across the grass and set down the box she was carrying. Whatever was inside tried to knock open the lid; Serena had to set a rock on top of it. She gazed down at the wolf with an expression somewhere between pity and disgust.

"I do believe you're right, Mr. Grobbs. I'd lost track of the days."

"Old Jack's draggin' somethin' terrible, ma'am."

She bent down and looked the creature in the eyes. Her fox wrap reared back, baring its teeth.

"Goodness me!" she said. "We'd better get him a drop of the Howling Moonbeast right away, don't you agree?"

"That'd be helpful, ma'am."

She reached under her wrap and lifted the gold chain

with the bottle from around her neck. I'd seen her take out this bottle before. Both times she'd waved it in front of Grobbs like she was lording it over him somehow.

She took another step toward the wolf, then stopped. She tilted her head and gave Grobbs a ponderous look.

"Just to be clear on our bargain, Mr. Grobbs. You've been doing a wonderful job keeping the road clear of the Strangle Oaks."

Grobbs nodded.

"Sister has a few complaints," said Serena, "but that's to be expected."

"It grieves me to hear so," said Grobbs. The look on his face said otherwise.

"And the boy," said Serena. "I know it's a nuisance having a child underfoot. But you're doing your best to keep watch of him, I hope?"

"Hardly ever leaves the woodshed," said Grobbs. "The boy won't make any trouble. I can promise you that."

She gave a satisfied nod. "I don't know what we'd do without you, Mr. Grobbs."

"Jack's ailin' pretty bad, Mizz Dredmoore. I'd be much obliged if you'd give him the tonic now, ma'am."

"Won't be long now, Mr. Grobbs, till we'll be able to fix up poor old Jack for good." She uncorked the bottle. "You help us get what we need from the boy, and Jack will be out chasing rabbits again in no time, just like the old days. Won't that be wonderful?"

"Yes'm," said Grobbs, in as agreeable a tone as he could

muster. But I could see a fearsome, deep hatred in his eyes. I had a hunch she could see it, too, though she sure didn't let on.

She knelt down in front of the wolf and poured two tiny drops right on the end of his nose. The creature began to shake something awful. His mouth foamed up and his eyes shot open, whether from fright or pain, I couldn't tell. Then he coughed out a steamy cloud of yellow breath and jumped upright with a start. He gave himself a violent shake. His ears stood straight. His eyes went sharp. He rose to his full height, hunchbacked and monstrous as ever.

Serena stepped away and put the stopper in the bottle. She dropped the necklace back under her fox wrap, which took a playful nip at her hand.

"Much obliged, ma'am." Grobbs petted the wolf, a look of relief in his eyes. "I'll see that the boy does as he's told."

With that, he turned and started down toward the marsh. Jack pounced along at his side, chomping the heads off daisies as he went.

I stayed out of sight until I was sure Serena had gone back to her morning doings. Then I raced down to the woodshed and sat on the stoop with my folks' letter. I was so jitter-fingered I couldn't get the envelope open.

What had happened back there between Serena and Grobbs? They had some kind of bargain. *Help us get what we need from the boy.* Serena used the potion to keep Grobbs's wolf alive, so long as he did what she said—and part of that was keeping an eye on me.

But only a few days ago, he'd told me to run away.

I tore open the envelope carefully, half expecting the letter to be some trick of my aunts'. But there in front of me, perfect as could be, was Poppers' squared-off writing.

DEAR ELIJAH,

YOUR MOTHER AND I MADE IT UP TO GREAT UNCLE EZRA'S PLACE IN THE TERRITORIES, BUT NO SIGN OF GRANDMA. THE GOOD NEWS IS THAT YOU GET TO STAY WITH YOUR AUNTS ANOTHER WEEK OR TWO.

MIND YOUR MANNERS AND DO WHATEVER YOUR AUNTS TELL YOU. IF THEY HAVE ANY SPECIAL REMEDIES OR TONICS THEY WANT YOU TO TAKE, JUST DO AS THEY SAY. YOUR MOTHER AND I GIVE THEM OUR COMPLETE TRUST. WE WILL FETCH YOU AS SOON AS WE CAN. OBEY YOUR AUNTS.

MUCH LOVE,
YOUR MOTHER & FATHER

I stared at the letter, a sick feeling deep in my chest.

If they have any special remedies . . . just do as they say.

How would Poppers know about that? Why would he mention such a thing? And why all the lecturing on being good and obedient?

Still . . . the handwriting was his, no question about it.

And Poppers was known for his sermonizing. . . .

"Is it good news?" came a voice from behind me.

I startled and dropped the letter on the ground. Then I turned to see Serena peering over my shoulder. I wondered how long she'd been there. Had she known I was watching from the window earlier? She had a worried look on her face, but it was a put-on kind of worry.

"Did they find Grandma Ester?" she asked.

"No." A wave of hopelessness stole over me. "They're going to keep looking."

"Poor Grandma Ester." Serena shook her head. "I guess we shouldn't be too surprised. Old age does terrible things to the mind."

She let out a sorrowful sigh.

"Well, she surely is lucky to have your folks looking out for her. Don't you worry, Elijah. I know your mother–she's as clever as they come. She'll get this all cleared up before you know it. You just wait and see."

She put a finger under my chin and tilted my head back. Her eyes took in my peeling blisters.

"Won't be long now," she said. "A little patience is all we need."

I wasn't sure whether she was talking about the pox on my face or my folks coming to fetch me. She hurried off toward the Snippers. The fox wrap leered back at me over her shoulder.

12

━◅◖◖◖◖◖◖◗◗◗◗◗◗▻━

The Burnt Broomstick

ONE OF MY CHORES WAS HAULING TRASH TO the dump wagon out in back of the barn. Agnes set out the Snippers rubbish every morning in old feed bags, and I'd roll it around back in a wheelbarrow. I always went slow and stuck to the chokecherry bushes as best I could, keeping an eye out for Grobbs and his wolf. Whenever the wagon filled up with garbage, he'd come hitch it up to his truck. Then he'd cart it off and dump it somewhere out in the marsh.

The day after I'd gotten the letter from Poppers, I was headed out to the dump wagon, sneaking my way through the chokecherries as usual, when I heard noises up ahead. Clanking and clattering sounds, like someone was rooting through the load of junk. I stopped dead and held my breath. If Grobbs and his hunchback wolf were at the wagon, I planned on heading in the other direction lickety-split. But the sound stopped. I inched my way forward till I got a clear peak at the wagon. Not a thing in sight. Not so much as a peep of noise. I'd probably just heard a crow rooting around in the rubbish, or maybe a squirrel. It was mortally shameful how every little thing set me on edge.

I looked around again to be double sure. Then I grabbed hold of the wheelbarrow and hurried up to the dump wagon. I tossed the sacks of trash up over the back gate as fast as I could. I was in such a hurry that one of the bags ripped open on the top of the gate and the rubbish spilled out. Most of it fell into the wagon, but a shower of ratty black feathers and a petrified rat tumbled down on top of me. I let out a scream and bumbled into the wheelbarrow. Then something else—a tattered piece of paper—came fluttering down through the air and landed at my feet. There were words scrawled across the top. I reached down and picked it up.

It was a map of Dredmoore Hollow.

Someone had drawn a picture of the road leading up to my house, and the wagon track out to the family graveyard. There was a fellow on horseback with a bat perched on his arm. The words DIG HERE were scrawled beneath him next to an inky black X. No matter the drawing was cock-eyed and scribbly, I knew right off what it was: the statue of my great-great-great grandpa Phineas Dredmoore. At the bottom of the map was some writing:

FIND all 5 pieces CAST IRON
BEWARE of BURROWING RAVENWEED!!!
Use Hoarfrost FUMIGATOR!!!

I recalled back to that stormy night I'd first seen Grobbs in the graveyard. I'd watched him use the Fumigator to freeze the Ravenweed solid, then dig in the very spot marked by the X. And I'd seen him drag five pieces of something heavy out of the ground.

If I'd had any doubts before, this was final proof Agnes and Serena were behind the whole thing. What was it he'd dug up from the graveyard? And why did my aunts want it so badly?

Another notion came over me: if someone had thrown the map in the trash, who knows what other telltales might be sitting up there in the wagon?

Cowardice and common sense told me to get out of there fast. Grobbs and his wolf could come by any minute. But I fought back my better judgment, clutched on to the back gate, and hurled myself up into the wagon.

What I saw in the bottom of that cart clobbered the wind right out of me. Nearly all the feed bags had been slashed open, and the floor was covered with ghastly horrors. Skulls and bones and withered claws. A dried-up frog the size of a woodchuck. The skeleton of a two-headed snake. A pair of gargantuan spiders that had been dipped in wax. And piled up in one corner: at least a dozen broomsticks, every last one of them charred and splintered.

I stood there in a shivering sweat, every muscle in my body tensed up and ready to run. All the times I'd hauled trash out here, I'd never climbed up and looked in the wagon. Not once. Never in my wildest notions would I have figured on anything like this.

A high-pitched shriek filled the air. From the corner of my eye, I saw a dark blur drop from the tree branches over my shoulder. Before I knew what hit me, I crashed to the floor. Something solid–a knee or an elbow, maybe–whacked me twice between the shoulder blades. The toe of a boot slammed into my ribs. I tried to pull away, rolling over just in time to see the handle of a broomstick go swishing past my ear.

I scrambled to my feet as a second blow flew at me. I threw up my hands, and by some miracle of luck, I grabbed hold of the bristles and held on tight.

"I know who you are!" screamed my attacker.

I was plenty surprised to see it was a girl. She tugged furiously at the broom handle.

"Witch boy!" she hissed through her teeth. "You and them Dredmoore sisters . . . you poisoned Clara!"

She was a scrawny little thing, probably about the same age as me, and dressed like a boy in ratty old knickers and a golf hat. A clump of frizzy hair hung over her eye. Her boots had no laces, and her face was smudged with dirt. I realized she was about the same size as the figure that I'd seen jump from the Runabout and burrow into the bushes the other day.

"I know what this stuff is!" She nodded toward the gruesome display in the bottom of the wagon. "I've got a jackknife, so you better not try your black magic on me!"

"I-I don't know what you're talking about," I said, struggling to keep a hold on my end of the broom.

It struck me that this girl was the only normal-looking person I'd seen lately at my aunts' place . . . and she had to live somewhere nearby. If I could only get her to stop trying to kill me, maybe she could help.

But before I could think of what to say, the girl went wild again. She lunged at me with a crazy shriek and knocked me against the side of the wagon. I hung on to the broom-stick for all I was worth.

"Calm down!" I shouted. "I want to help you . . . honest. Just tell me who Clara is."

She gritted her teeth and kicked me square in the shin. I let out a howl and sprang back, ripping the broom right out of her hands. A rush of anger came over me. It was like heat. Like fire shooting up a chimney. I'd never felt anything like it before. And at that very moment, the broom burst into flames.

The girl staggered backward, gasping.

I screamed and let go of the broomstick, fire licking at my face and fingers. . . .

But the broom didn't fall to the ground.

It hung there . . . bobbing in the air . . . fire and smoke spouting from both ends.

The girl and I clung to the side of the wagon, both of us too transfixed to make a sound. The broomstick wavered eerily, black smoke billowing into the air. Then, suddenly, its handle tilted upward and it shot off into the sky. It bolted straight toward the sun till it was high over the barn roof. Then it turned, swirling out of control, and pitched back toward the ground. It disappeared over the front side of the barn.

A moment later, we heard a thunderous *SMASH!* The sound of shattering glass—most likely one of the Snippers' windows.

Grobbs's wolf broke into a frenzy of howls . . . followed by the sound of the Snippers' door bursting open and a commotion of shouting voices.

I turned to look at the girl, but she'd disappeared. All I saw was a shadow slipping into the bullrush at the edge of the marsh.

It occurred to me I ought to run for it, too. I leaped from the wagon, catching my foot on the latch. The gate fell open, and I tumbled to the ground—with the entire load of rubbish thundering down on top of me.

A big hand grabbed hold of my arm and dragged me out of the heap. The foul smell of licorice root told me who it was. The hunchback wolf stared me in the eye and gave a murderous growl, froth dripping from his fangs. Then Agnes yanked me out of Grobbs's grip and glared at me with her purple eyes, so mad she couldn't talk.

Serena surveyed the mess with an icy quiet. Charred skulls and bones lay scattered on the ground all around me. Toad skins, broomsticks, a shattered box full of withered bat wings.

"I . . . I was just throwing rubbish in the wagon." My voice sounded like a choking cricket. "And the gate fell open."

"Get to the woodshed," said Serena in a dangerous tone. Her fox wrap bared its pointy teeth, the glass eyes gone to slits.

"I'll clean it up," I said. "It won't take long. . . ."

I snatched a red rag from the pile, as if I meant to start picking up the mess that very moment. Serena's eyes widened, and she grabbed the rag out of my hand. Then she slipped it behind her back.

"You've done enough already!" Her one sharp tooth bit into her bottom lip so hard that a drop of blood trickled out.

I saw Agnes move behind her. The red cloth disappeared into Agnes's parasol. There was something disturbingly familiar about that rag. It was made of red flannel and came to a point on one end, with a white tassel hanging off.

Just like my father's nightcap.

My skin went cold.

Agnes and Serena glared down at me, their eyes as dark as doom.

13

Runabout Runaway

I took it for a bad sign when I woke up and discovered the woodshed door was locked. It had been a few nights since my aunts had bothered with the padlock–and they'd always sent Grobbs to set me loose in the morning.

Not today.

Maybe this was the day they'd been waiting for . . . the day they'd finally do whatever it was they were planning for me.

I was already a quivering wreck, and the locked door didn't help matters. I'd been awake most of the night, pondering the events at the dump wagon. The crazy girl who'd jumped me. The broomstick that burst into flames. And worst of all, the red flannel cloth that looked just like Poppers' nightcap.

I tried to convince myself that I was letting my imagination get carried away again. That flannel rag could've come from most anywhere.

But what if that rag *was* Poppers' nightcap? What in kingdom come was it doing here?

One thing was clear as daylight: it was foolish of me to sit and wait any longer for my parents to come rescue me. There was no telling what my aunts were up to, or what they'd done. I had to get out . . . get away from Moaning Marsh . . . no matter what.

It took me the better part of an hour to pull a board off one of the windows using a leg of the cot for a pry bar. Then I raced up the hill toward the Magic Snippers. I hid in a big clump of lilacs near the dead butternut tree. If I wasn't jittered enough already, there was a damp wind blowing that morning, and it cut right through me, making my teeth chatter something furious.

Maybe an hour later, a sputtery engine made its way across Moaning Marsh and rolled up over the hill. The girls parked the Runabout up next to the Snippers and headed for the door, same as always. The usual swarm of toads lolloped after them.

I waited a couple minutes to be safe; then I hurried over and peered into the back of the truck. I was in luck for once. There was an old horse blanket spread out across a pile of hay, with a pair of old boots and some rope poking out. Plenty of room for me. My plan was to stow away in the pickup box, and once the girls drove back to wherever they were going—hopefully someplace in Blossom Springs—I'd jump out and run for all I was worth.

If I could've come up with a better plan, I sure as Christmas would've used it. Who could guess how long those girls might be inside the Snippers? Or what ghastly things my aunts would do to them before they came out again?

Anyhow . . . I'd made up my mind: this was the best chance I had.

I climbed into the truck bed as quiet as I could. Then I wriggled under the blanket and burrowed my way into the hay.

My foot bumped something soft and lumpy. I tried to shove it out of the way with my boot, and a shout rang out.

"Aaaaagh!"

The blanket shot up out of the hay, and something smacked me right between the eyes. I reeled backward and nearly toppled out of the pickup box. Before I could come to my senses, the blanket sailed toward me again, this time catching me hard in the gut.

I let out a gasp and doubled over.

The thing jumped on top of me and pummeled my back and head, pinning me facedown in the straw.

An arm slid 'round my neck, putting me in a stranglehold, and a voice hissed into my ear.

"Don't try nothing or I'll break your neck!"

A girl's voice.

"You're that Dredmoore boy," she said. "The one from the dump wagon."

She grabbed hold of my hair and pulled me around to

face her. Her face was smudged with dirt, same as the last time I'd seen her, when she came at me with the broomstick. Her hat had come off, and her hair stuck out in a great frizzy spray all around her head.

"You ain't very tough, are you?" she said, squinting hard at me.

"No," I groaned. It felt like she was going to tear my scalp off. "You're pulling out my hair!"

"What're you doing in my sister's truck?"

"I was trying to sneak a ride." I pried at her fingers, but she had a grip like a bear trap. "Trying to run away . . ."

She let loose, and I toppled over into the hay. I lay there groaning and rubbing my scalp for a minute before she grabbed the front of my shirt.

"You got to the count of three to tell me what you and those Dredmoore sisters've been doing to Clara." She held her fist up to my nose. "You better talk quick."

"Take it easy! Which one's Clara?"

"You know who she is! The skinny one with the hat that keeps floating off her head!"

"She's your sister?" I eyed the girl over, catching my breath. The gal with the floating hat had been all done up in frills and makeup–whereas this girl with her knuckles in my face was part tomboy, part bobcat.

"I've seen her go into the Magic Snippers with those other two," I said.

"That's Dora White and Mabel Flanders."

"My aunts keep them in there for hours. One time they

stayed all night. I've got no idea what they do in there, but I'm pretty sure it's why your sister's . . . *changed*."

The girl lowered her fist a notch, but her eyes stayed fierce as ever.

"I tried to talk to your sister and her friends," I went on. "I tried to warn them . . . stop them from going into the Snippers. But they attacked me. Mostly that short one . . . the one with all the toads."

"Mabel." The girl lowered her fist a bit farther. "She's always been kind of mean and sneaky. But the toads . . ."

"I know," I said. "There's plenty of things like that going on around here. Weird, creepy stuff . . . like the junk in that dump wagon . . . like that flying broomstick that went up in flames."

The girl narrowed her eyes and looked me over, as if she was pondering whether or not to trust me.

"Tell you what I think," she said at last. "I think your aunts are witches."

I nodded. "I can't see any other explanation for it. That's why I was trying to run away."

The girl let go of my shirt and dropped back in the hay. She gave the Snippers' door a hateful glare.

"So how long have you lived here . . . with *them*?"

"I don't live here. I never even met them before this summer," I said. "And I wish I never had. Me and my folks live down south near Cold Creek Junction. They're Mama's sisters. But she never talked about them. Now I guess I know why."

"My name's Dez." She held out her hand.

"I'm Elijah." She had a solid handshake. I had a hunch more than one boy had been clobbered with that hand.

"I think I saw you a couple days ago," I said. "You jumped from the truck and disappeared into the bushes."

Dez nodded. "I've been tagging along, hiding in the truck. Trying to figure out what's going on up here. Clara and her friends weren't the first ones. They just got it worse than anyone else."

She told me how Agnes and Serena had come around Blossom Springs after they first opened up shop five years ago, handing out coupons for free beauty treatments. Everybody that made the trip out to the Magic Snippers ended up with all their hair falling out a few days later. Their scalps turned as orange as pumpkins, and their words came out backward for the next few weeks. After that, folks stayed clear of the Snippers. Grobbs went around door-to-door, giving away bottles of special hair tonic and skin softeners, and things like that. But if anybody dared to use the stuff, Dez had never heard about it. A couple months ago, two of Dez's neighbors, Eva and Erma Bumperly, made the drive out to Moaning Marsh. They weren't exactly what you'd call good-looking gals. So when they came back looking like they'd just won a beauty pageant, news got around fast. Nobody seemed to pay much notice to the girls' sudden change in temperament—from mousy to monstrous—except Mr. Bumperly, who never let them near the Snippers again.

That's when Clara, Dora, and Mabel made their first trip

out–though nobody knew it at the time. Two days later Clara came home in the middle of the night looking so pretty, Dez said, that you'd have thought she was a different person. But she acted queer in the head–all dazed, as if she was in a trance. And mean-tempered, too. Clara wouldn't say where she'd been, and if anybody asked, she went into a rage, throwing books and boots, whatever happened to be in reach. Later that night, Dez spied her down in the root cellar, filling up a jar with spider legs–which she got by plucking them off with her teeth. Dez snuck into Clara's bedroom and found a sack full of odd things: dried-up frogs, a hornet's nest, a sock full of pig's teeth, a pair of her pa's suspenders, and a clump of stinging nettles. The next time Clara drove up to the Snippers, Dez snuck along in the back of the Runabout to find out what was going on.

"When you and me met up in that dump wagon full of witching stuff," she said, "I figured you were in on it–the dark magic, I mean. I was fixing to get some kind of proof. A witching stick, or some head-shrinking potion, or something like that. Then I'd take it to the police and they'd have to believe me. But when that broomstick caught fire and went flying off, I ran away before I could get ahold of anything to show."

"Let me stay here and hide with you," I said. "After Clara gets done, we can go over to that police station, and I'll tell them everything I've seen."

"They won't believe a word of it," said Dez. "We're just kids. We need *proof*."

"I'll show them these fish scales on my chin. My aunts call them Piscatory Pox. See?"

She leaned closer and squinted. "They look like plain old scabs to me."

I ran my fingertips over my chin. She was right. The scales had finally healed over. I could hardly even feel them anymore.

"There's got to be something we can do. I don't know what my aunts are up to . . . but I know it's bad."

Then I told her the whole story, starting with the night Grobbs showed up at the graveyard, right up to the day she met me in the dump wagon. I told her about the odd tonics and remedies Agnes and Serena used on me, and how they were so infernally fixed on my chin.

Dez leaned in and squinted at my jaw.

"They hate me," I said. "I can tell. They'd just as soon I was dead, especially Agnes. If I could only figure out what it is they want from me."

"You got no idea at all?"

I shook my head. "I heard them say something about a curse . . . and what they called the Dredmoore gift. But I can't make any sense of it."

Both of us stared at the Magic Snippers' door, mulling the situation in silence for a while. It was good to have somebody on my side for a change—somebody who knew that things weren't right. I'd been starting to wonder if I was going crazy.

"Yesterday," I said, "after you ran away from the dump

wagon, I picked up an old rag from the rubbish heap—it was a red flannel nightcap, just like my father wears. He was wearing it the night he and Mama disappeared."

Her eyes widened in shock. "You think the Dredmoore sisters murdered your folks?"

The question was like a smack in the gut.

"M-m-murdered? Why would they . . . ?"

"No, no," she said, waving her hands in the air like she was trying to take it back. "I'm sure they didn't murder no one. I was just—"

"Mama and Poppers sent a letter," I said desperately. "It was my father's handwriting—"

"Right, right!" she said. "That was stupid of me. I shouldn't have said it."

She grabbed my arm, all flustered and awkward, and she started petting my hand like I was a frightened puppy. It was a clumsy thing to do, but I liked her for it. And after a bit, I calmed down some. My head started to clear again.

"We need to find something to show the police back in Blossom Springs," she said. "Something so strange and bewitched that there's no way to deny it."

She leaned against the side of the pickup box and stared at the house with a scary gleam in her eye.

"Do you still have any of those remedies the sisters gave you? That beetle silk or the fish powder?"

I shook my head. "It all got tossed into the marsh."

"What's in the house? Do they have another one of those flying brooms? Or a witching stick or something?"

"Not that I ever saw lying around," I said. "That stuff in the wagon was the first I'd ever seen–and Grobbs dumped it all in the swamp. Aunt Agnes had a witching stick, but–"

"There's got to be something," Dez said.

"I think they do all their witching out in the barn," I said. "Or maybe in some of their secret rooms. But don't you think we should go get some help before–"

"Secret rooms?"

"They keep most of the rooms in the house locked up. I'm only allowed in the kitchen, the pantry, and the water closet."

"Hot dandy!" Dez slapped me hard on the shoulder. "I bet there's heaps of witching stuff in those rooms!"

"Could be," I said. "But they're all locked up."

She reached into her pocket and pulled out a handful of snipped-off wires and half a dozen skeleton keys.

"What're those for?" I asked.

"They're for picking locks." She gave me a sly grin. "That's what I was planning to do as soon as Clara went into the Snippers. I learned how from a book."

"But Agnes and Serena–"

"They'll be working on Clara and the others for at least a couple hours, I bet."

I glanced around, my brain racing for some way to talk her out of this.

"What about Grobbs? And that hunchback wolf of his?" I asked.

She leaped out of the truck and tucked her hair up under her golf hat.

"Are you coming or not?"

I stared at her in disbelief. Was she really fool enough to run straight into my aunts' house and start picking locks?

"All right," she said. "I'll be back. You better stay hid under the horse blanket."

Next thing I knew she was galloping across the barnyard, headed right for the house.

I sat there for a second, dumbfounded, watching her scamper over the grass. Then I jumped out of the truck and ran after her.

14

Thunder Bludgeon

THERE WERE TWO THINGS I COULD SEE RIGHT off about Dez. She wasn't afraid of anything. And once she got a notion into her head, there was no talking her out of it. She bolted toward my aunts' front porch in such a tizzy, I expected her to kick the door down.

"Hold up!" I hollered after her as loud as I dared.

She turned and let me catch up, and I dragged her behind a pile of old barn boards.

"Not the front door." I tried to catch my breath. "There's another way . . . out back."

A loud clanking sound came from the side of the barn. We both turned to see Grobbs banging away on the front of his truck with a pipe wrench. His hunchback wolf was sniffing all around the bushes like he'd picked up a scent—I hoped it wasn't us.

"This is no good," I whispered to Dez. "Grobbs is too close. He might see us."

"Then go back and wait in the truck. I'll be done before you know it."

She slapped me on the back and bolted off toward the far side of the house. It was infuriating how stubborn that girl was. I clenched my teeth and ran after her.

Dez slipped through that back door smooth as a breeze, and went straight to work snooping around and jiggling doorknobs. She fixed on the door nearest the parlor, the one that Serena was always sneaking through. It was locked as usual. Dez pulled out her gadgets and took a long skeleton key from the bunch.

"This ought to do it."

"I don't think that's going to work," I said. "There's a whole bunch of pins in there with little springs behind them, and you've got to–"

Dez shoved the key into the lock and started twisting it around like she was trying to bust a hole through to the other side. Her face scrunched up in concentration. She breathed so hard her nose made a whistling sound.

I had a fairly clear notion of how a plug-and-pin lock worked, and I could see right off that Dez had never picked open a real lock in her life. Suddenly the key stuck on something.

"Ha!" Her face lit up.

I peeked out the porch door, worried she might've drawn some attention.

"Now all I got to do . . . is give it . . . just the right . . . *twist!*" She gave the key a sharp turn.

Just then, an awful *snap!* came from inside the keyhole.

"It . . . it broke!" Dez pulled the skeleton key out of the hole. It was snapped off in the middle.

"Never mind the lock," I said. "Let's get back to the truck before somebody comes."

Too late. The front door banged open. The sound of high-heeled shoes clattered toward us down the hall. I grabbed Dez's arm and dragged her stumbling into the larder. We squeezed in between a couple of flour barrels, and I signaled for her to keep quiet.

The high heels clip-clopped right past us to the other side of the kitchen, stopping in front of the door with the broken key. There were some jingling sounds. Then the door rattled as somebody tried to work the lock.

"Miserable rotten thing . . ."

It was Agnes.

She rattled harder, now cursing and banging at the door with her parasol.

"Old wreck of a farmhouse!"

I could hear her rustling around inside her purse, or maybe her parasol.

"Fine time for this," she muttered. "Now I'll have to hear it from Sister. . . ."

Then came a soft tapping sound, like she was rapping a stick against the door, and she called out something that sounded like–

"Hag's Hammer!"

An ear-splitting noise shook the walls. It was loud as a

thunderclap. Flour and dust sprinkled down on Dez and me from the shelves above. A smell filled the air—the stench of rotten eggs and smoke.

Dez and I looked at each other, gasping, both thinking the same thing: *Agnes had bewitched the door open!*

"Well, there's a pretty mess!" she snarled. "Can't even conjure a door open without that confounded curse fouling it up."

I heard her footsteps move farther away—into the open room, I reckoned. There was some banging around and some more cussing and muttering. Then the footsteps moved back across the kitchen floor and down the hallway to the front door.

"Mr. Grobbs! We'll need a new door to the library. The old one needs burning. You best do it *now*."

"I'll get to it," he hollered back from somewhere outside.

"Your truck can wait!" she shouted.

"Your infernal door can wait!" said Grobbs.

There was an icy pause.

"I got customers to mind," said Agnes. "You just make sure you take care of it before I come back, you hear?"

"Don't you worry, Mizz Dredmoore," answered Grobbs with equal snippiness. "I got it at the top o' my list."

"Sister'll hear about this," she said. "You'd be wise to watch your tongue. It'd be a pity for ol' Jack if that Moonbeast Tonic dried up."

Grobbs let out a dismissive snort.

The sound of Agnes's heels clopped across the front

porch and down the steps. The front door banged shut.

"C'mon," whispered Dez. "Let's get a look at that bewitched door."

She jumped out from behind the flour barrels. I stumbled after her.

"Grobbs'll be here any second," I said. "Don't you think we should—"

We both stopped in the middle of the kitchen. The *thing* in front of us looked nothing like a door now. It had swelled up to the shape of a gnarly old tree—roots, branches, and all—sawed off at the top where it squeezed into the door jamb. Ragged bark hung all around it. The branches were coiled up like snakes and thorny as briar vines. The smell of wood rot filled the room. I could hear a sound, too. A low, hollow groan that shuddered through the walls and floor.

I backed away as fast as I could, tugging Dez by her shirt-tail. She was transfixed by the thing.

"C'mon!"

"Why would your aunt turn a door into . . . *this?*"

"Didn't you hear her?" I said, trying to drag Dez away. "She said something about that *curse* again. . . . That's what made her conjuring go wrong. Now could we please—"

"Look!" shouted Dez. She broke free of my grip and ran toward the bewitched door.

"Careful!" I cried.

There was a broken stick on the floor in the unlocked room, just the other side of the beastly door. One end of the stick was burnt. The other had a small bone tied to it. This had to be Agnes's witching stick. It must've busted in two when she conjured the spell.

"Hot dandy!" cried Dez, stepping toward the stick. "If we can make it conjure something, we can show the police and–"

The door let out a thundering growl. Half a dozen limbs uncoiled and shot out like whips. Dez reeled back, trying to escape, but the briary branches snagged hold of her shirt and trousers.

"Dez!"

I lunged and grabbed hold of her, wild and clumsy, banging my head into hers. We both went tumbling into the dark room beyond. A flurry of thorny branches came snapping after us. We scrambled out of the way . . . deeper into the room.

Some of the branches had snapped off. They clung to Dez's clothes, twitching and writhing like eels out of water.

"They're biting me!" she shrieked, swatting at herself.

I whacked and slapped at her sleeves and trousers, just as panicked as she was, until the last prickly piece fell away. Then we both ran to the farthest corner and dropped to the floor, clutching each other. The bewitched door heaved back and forth on its hinges, trying to break loose. Branches slashed at the air. A deep growl rumbled through the room, shaking the walls. Then, with one fierce final swing, the monstrous thing slammed itself into the doorway and the room went dark.

I read in *Farmer's Almanac* once that only fools and bedbugs go where they're not welcome. That's good sound advice, but I don't suppose those almanac folks ever spent much time with my new friend, Dez. If we'd only stayed hidden under that horse blanket like I wanted, everything would've been fine, and we'd be on our way to Blossom Springs in no time. Instead, there we were, huddled together in a dark corner of my aunts' secret library, held prisoner by a man-eating tree. . . .

After a while, my eyes got used to the dark and I spotted an oil lamp on a table. I was reluctant to move from my spot for worry of what other ghastly aberrations Agnes and Serena might have skulking around the place. Dez seemed to have lost a bit of her moxie, too. All of a sudden she realized she was clinging to my arm and let go. She stood up and checked herself for leftover thorns.

The girl was prepared for most anything, I'll give her that much. In her pocket, she had a flint and steel, plus matches. We lit the oil lamp and picked our way around the library, slow and nervous. Nearly every wall was covered with bookshelves, most of them empty. The place was dusty and draped heavy with cobwebs. It smelled of damp and mold.

The main thing in the room was an old writing table, piled high with raggedy books and papers. Behind the table was an empty fireplace. A pair of boars' heads were mounted over the mantel, cobwebs hanging from their tusks. There were boarded-up windows on either side of the flue. As far as I could see, there was no other way in or out of the place. I threw a skittish glance back at the bewitched door. It stood there, heaving ever so slightly—its thorny branches curled up tight—lying in wait. A deep, soft rumbling sound moved through the walls and floor.

"I bet there's a secret passage," said Dez. She rapped on walls and poked at the woodwork eagerly. "Witch houses always have secret passages. I've seen it in loads of picture shows. There's trap doors and hidden stairways and tunnels full of vampire bats."

After everything that had happened at my aunts' place, it didn't seem far-fetched that there'd be tunnels full of bats hidden behind the walls. I wasn't so sure I cared to find them, though. I set my attention on the boarded-up windows next to the flue. They were sealed shut with old paint. We'd have to break the glass, then knock the window boards off to get out that way. Not exactly subtle.

"Look at this old writing quill!" Dez stood at the desk, holding up a long black feather with a piece of red cloth tied down near the nub. "I wonder if they use it for some kind of witching spells?"

She grabbed a piece of paper and started scratching away on it with the quill.

"You have to dip it in ink first," I said. "But let's not—"

"*Oh!*" Dez pulled back her hand and let go of the quill as if it had bit her. We both watched as the feather stood upright on its own, tip-down on the paper. It danced across the sheet, writing in quick movements:

You have to dip it in ink first. But let's not

Dez gave the feather a nudge, and it toppled over. I held up the paper for a closer look and a sickening chill rushed over me.

"That looks just like my Poppers' handwriting. . . ."

Dez stared at me in confusion.

A terrible thought hit me.

"Dez . . ." My voice quavered. "Try it again."

She lifted the quill from the paper and held it tip-down on the page, then let go. The pen stood on its own.

I leaned closer, speaking as slow and clear as I could, though my voice shook something awful. Even so, the quill marched across the page, every word a perfect imitation of Poppers' squared-off penmanship. Exactly like the letter Agnes gave me:

DEAR ELIJAH,
YOUR MOTHER AND I MADE IT UP TO GREAT UNCLE EZRA'S PLACE

Dez and I stared down at the paper. The quill stood at attention, motionless, waiting for the next word.

"That's . . . that's his writing?" she asked quietly. The pen scribbled out the words just like she spoke them.

I nodded, silent and numb.

I lifted the feather and looked at the strip of red cloth tied above the nub. It was red flannel . . . just like the rag Serena had snatched from my hands out by the dump wagon.

My legs went weak.

"What is it?" said Dez. "Is that . . . ?"

"It's a piece of my father's nightcap," I said, my voice hoarse. "The one from the dump wagon. It must be part of a spell. . . ."

A sharp noise rang out from behind us. *WHACK!*

The bewitched door let out a beastly shriek, and the branches came thrashing to life. On the other side of the door came the sound again. *WHACK! WHACK! WHACK!*

The violent blows of ax against wood.

Grobbs!

15

Out of the Ashes

"WE'LL HAVE TO SMASH OUT THROUGH A window," said Dez. Her face was red. I couldn't tell whether she was excited or scared.

She lifted her golf cap and stuck the magic quill into her hair. Then she snatched up a chair from next to the writing desk and hoisted it over her head like she was about to heave it through the window.

"Wait!" I cried. "If we break that glass, Grobbs will know we're in here. We'll never get the window boards off in time."

She gave me an impatient glare.

WHACK! WHACK! WHACK! sang Grobbs's ax. A frightful wail shook the house. Branches slashed wildly at the air.

"He doesn't know we're in here yet," I said. I studied the room desperately. My eye fell on the chimney bricks. "We could hide. We could crawl up the flue."

I knelt down so I could get a look up the chimney, and

my heart sunk. There was a thick slab of iron up there blocking the way.

"No good," I said. "It's blocked."

I started to back out of the hearth, wiping the ashes from my knees, when something in the rear of the fireplace caught my eye.

WHACK! WHACK! THUMP! The bewitched door let out one last ghastly howl . . . and then went silent.

Dez snatched up two fire pokers—heavy iron and black with soot.

"You better take one of these!" she said. "If we both charge him—"

"There's a cinder door in the back of the fireplace," I whispered. "For digging out the ashes from outside."

Dez crouched down in the ashes next to me. She let out a soft whistle.

It was a small door made of rusty iron. It looked like it was probably big enough so Dez and I could squeeze through.

Probably.

A heavy *THUD* shook the room. Then another . . .

"Grobbs is trying to kick the door open!" cried Dez.

There was a pair of andirons in the bottom of the fireplace, cradling some charred logs. I dragged them out onto the floor and gave the metal door a shove. It didn't budge.

Grobbs's heavy boot thundered away. *BOOM! BOOM! BOOM!* The oil lamp flickered. Ashes showered down on me from the flue.

I heard Grobbs curse from the other side of the door.

"Hand me that fire poker," I whispered to Dez, a dry lump in my throat.

"Move over!" She shoved me aside. "I'll kick it open."

"No . . ." I tried to hold her back. "Don't make too much noi–"

She leaped in feetfirst and gave the cinder door a wild kick with the heel of her boot. It swung open and banged against the chimney bricks with a steely clang.

She turned to me with a cocky grin.

"Ho there!" shouted Grobbs. "Who's in that room?"

Dez's smirk faded.

"Hurry!" I pushed her toward the hole. "You first!"

She turned and plunged headfirst into the opening. She squirmed and wriggled. Her boots kicked up a cloud of ashes in my face and I fell back coughing.

A new sound rang out. *CLANK! CLANK! CLANK!* Steel against steel. Then the noise of something metal clattering to the floor.

Grobbs was knocking the pins out of the hinges!

Once he got all three hinges out that door would come down, easy as pie.

Dez had made it halfway through. She was stuck at the hips and her two feet were kicking up a whirlwind of ashes. Grobbs would be through that door any second.

It wasn't very gentleman-like, but I dove into that fireplace and grabbed hold of Dez's backside with both hands. Then I shoved for all I was worth. With one sudden lurch, her bottom squeezed through the hole and she dropped to the outside.

CLANK! CLANK! CLINGGGGG!

Two hinges gone—just one more to go.

I plunged into the hole headfirst, the same as Dez . . . but then I realized that if I left those andirons sitting out on the floor, Grobbs would figure out where we'd gone and be after us in no time.

Dez grabbed hold of my head, ready to pull me out like she was birthing a calf.

"Hold on," I said with a grunt. "Got to . . . get the andirons."

"No time for that . . ." she started.

But I pulled free and twisted myself around in the ashes. I grabbed hold of the irons and dragged them into the fireplace. I stuck my feet out through the cinder door, meaning to work my way backward, pulling the andirons along with me. But they were too heavy.

CLANK! CLANK! CLINGGGGG!

The last hinge fell to the floor.

I glanced up, frozen stiff with panic. It was too late to do anything. The door shook and snapped loose from its hinges. Then, slowly, horribly, it started falling into the room.

At exactly that moment, Dez gave a powerful tug on both of my ankles and I shot backward out the cinder door, dragging the andirons with me. I let go of them at the last minute and dropped to the ground . . . right on top of Dez. An explosive crash echoed from inside the house as the bewitched door hit the floor.

I scrambled to my feet and pushed the cinder door shut as gently as I could.

Grobbs's voice rattled the windows. "Is that you, boy? I know you're in here!"

Dez and I ran all the way to Clara's truck without so much as a glance behind us.

16

―――⟨⟩―――

The Witching Maids

DEZ AND I LAY QUIET AS LOGS UNDER THE HORSE blanket in the back of Clara's truck. My heart was still motoring away in my chest after that close call. No doubt, Grobbs and his hunchback wolf were out tracking us that very moment.

The wind had kicked up something fierce. It was making such a racket that I could hardly hear myself think. If Grobbs snuck up on us now, we'd never hear him coming.

Dez didn't seem the least bit rattled. She raised the blanket and pulled the magic quill out from under her hat. "Wait till the Blossom Springs police see this! I bet they'll send every sheriff in the state up here!"

I nodded and tried to smile.

"What's the matter?" she asked. Then she glanced down at the quill and ran a finger over the red cloth. "Oh . . . You think they . . . did something to your pa?"

Her face was shadowy blue in the dim light beneath the blanket.

I took a big breath. My head felt foggy.

"They might've just snuck it from his bedroom," she said.

I shrugged. "Anyway . . . I'll just be glad when Clara gets back so we can go fetch help."

Dez threw the blanket back and pulled herself up to the edge of the pickup box. The wind was howling away to beat all. It knocked off her golf hat and whipped her hair into a bushy tangle.

"Wonder what's taking her so long?" She frowned at the Snippers' front door. "She's been in there two hours, easy."

She dropped back into the truck bed and spread the horse blanket over us again.

"Are you and Clara pretty close?" I asked.

She scrunched up her mouth and shook her head.

"Used to be. Back when we were little."

Our breath made it damp and warm under the blanket. Stuffy and nice at the same time.

"When Clara got older, she changed," said Dez. "Got all full of herself. Like she was better than everybody else–her and those friends of hers, Dora and Mabel. She went boy crazy, too. She'd giggle and tease them, and then, soon as they came calling, she'd act disgusted and tell them to go jump in a lake."

Dez smiled at this last part, then turned serious. "She was always kind of pretty, I reckon. Not all frizzy haired and tomboy like me."

She looked me in the eye. "I got no use for boys most of the time. The smart ones know enough to keep their distance."

I rubbed the bump over my eye where she'd slugged me earlier.

"I must not be one of the smart ones," I said.

We both laughed.

Little by little, the daylight faded till Dez and I could barely see each other under the horse blanket. Dez peaked out of the pickup box every couple minutes, getting more fidgety each time. No sign of Clara . . . no sign of anyone. I knew what was coming next, even before Dez spoke the words.

"I'm going to go see if I can peek in a window or something."

"They're boarded up," I said.

"Maybe there's a crack somewhere." Dez jumped out of the truck bed.

There was no point in arguing; I'd learned that much about Dez by now. Besides, I knew she was right. It'd been too long—we had to do something. I took a quick look around for Grobbs, then hopped out of the pickup box and followed after her.

Our feet had hardly hit the ground when the Snippers' door swung open. Dez sprang back in surprise and we clobbered heads. We both muffled our groans and sprang for the nearest patch of bushes—a thick clump of ragweed and thistles.

"That short one, Mabel, showed good promise today," said Serena in an excited voice. "I do believe she's got some natural gift–the way she conjured the pitchfork to fly at that big one!"

"Those other two are about as bright as a clump of sod," Agnes groused. "It took the giant one five tries to tie that swatch of flannel onto the Mimicker's Quill."

Dez and I peeked out through a tangle of toothy leaves as the sisters sauntered toward us. I held my breath. Pricker-bushes jabbed at my neck and arms.

"No matter," said Serena. "It's too late to hunt for new witching maids now. All we need them to do is fetch things and mix some ingredients. Mabel can mix up the Mending Brew."

"I don't trust her," said Agnes. "That look in her eyes. And the way all those toads follow her around."

Serena laughed. "I'm proud of our little Mabel. You'll see–after we get what we need from the boy, our witching maids can do the rest."

"I hope you're right," said Agnes. "Are you sure the boy's pox are healed up enough?"

"Well now, Sister," Serena replied in a mocking tone. "It seems that *your* Piscatory Pox have cleared away quite nicely. And if I recall correctly, you contracted your affliction the exact same time as our nephew, didn't you?"

Agnes stopped walking. Serena paused, too, and gazed wistfully up at the orange moon. Her fox wrap raised its withered head and glanced around, sniffing suspiciously. Dez and I looked at each other, certain the thing had picked up our scent. It snapped a moth out of the air, then tucked its head back under Serena's chin.

"I told Grobbs to keep the boy locked up," said Serena. "Everything should be ready for tomorrow."

She started walking toward the house again. "Remember, Sister . . . you leave everything to me this time. We've waited too long for this. The last thing we need is another one of your blunders."

Agnes snorted in outrage, jabbing her parasol into the ground. A flash of purple sparks burst from the tip, and all around her, the grass turned to writhing black worms.

Serena chuckled and shook her head. "My point exactly, Agnes dear."

They said some other things I couldn't make out. Then the front door of the house banged shut.

All the color had gone out of Dez's face. "Did you hear what they said about my sister and her friends? They called them *witching maids*! They're going to use them for . . . some kind of conjuring . . ."

I nodded. "Mending Brew, they called it."

"And you, too!" cried Dez, her eyes full of worry. "They think you're locked in the woodshed, and tomorrow they'll–"

She stopped and her jaw went tight. A look stole over her face–that same look I'd seen in the dump wagon, and again in the back of Clara's truck: fierce and fearless, a girl who would never back down.

A girl who just might get us killed.

ᏇᎳᎪ

Dez tried every lock pick in her pocket on the Snippers' door with no luck. She finally gave up, and we smashed the boards off one of the barn windows with a rock. We climbed in through the busted pane.

The sharp smell of soap, or maybe perfume, stung the inside of my nose. A gurgling slurping sound came from somewhere off in the darkness. We lit a couple of Dez's matches and searched around till we found a kerosene lantern.

By the looks of it, we'd broken into some sort of storage room. Cockeyed shelves lined the walls, cluttered with jars and bottles. The labels were scrawled with frightful names–*Cackleworms, Scab Root,* and *Drowned Man's Eyeballs.* Two cow stalls had been turned into bins filled up with gnarled roots and withered mushrooms. There were crates overflowing with beastly skulls, blackened bones, tusks, and tails. Herbs and weeds had been strung from the ceiling to dry. Black goop dripped from a toadstool the size of a frying pan, leaving a puddle that bubbled and smoldered on the floor.

Dez found a pile of broomsticks in one corner of the room. They looked as if they'd been pulled out of a bonfire, all charred and splintered, the straw bristles burned down to black nubs. She grabbed one and straddled it like a hobbyhorse.

"I bet it'll fly if you're a witch," she whispered.

I was anxious for her to get off the thing before it burst into flames like the one in the dump wagon.

A dim light spilled in through a doorway at the far end of the room. The gurgling slurping sound seemed to be coming from that direction. I signaled to Dez. She nodded. We crept up to the door, cracked it open, and peeked through.

Both of us had to muffle a gasp.

Clara, Mabel, and Dora were strapped into chairs in the middle of the beauty shop. Each of them had a cloth sack over her head, with a little round window so they could see out. A jumble of hoses sprouted from each sack, making it look as if the girls were being attacked by a mechanical octopus. The hoses hooked into a black stovepipe that hung from the ceiling, heaving and swaying, and making a frightful racket. Puffs of green smoke poured from holes in the contraption, surrounding the girls in a pea-colored fog. A small army of toads sprawled on the floor at Mabel's feet.

"*Clar–!*" Dez started to shout, but I clapped my hand over her mouth and dragged her back into the storage room.

She walloped me in the ribs with her elbow and tried to shake me off. I hung on tight, gasping for air.

"That's witching potion!" Dez reeled around and glared at me. "They're poisoning her!"

"Wait, Dez!" I said, doubled over and wheezing. "Let's think first . . . a plan . . ."

She let out an impatient snort and nodded.

I stepped between her and the doorway, just in case. "Those girls have been potioned pretty badly by now. Especially that one with the toads . . . Mabel. You heard what Serena said about her. . . . She might be dangerous."

"I ain't leaving here without my sister," said Dez.

"Okay," I said. "We'll get Clara out of here—but only Clara. Then we can send help . . . a sheriff or somebody . . . to come back for Dora and Mabel."

Dez peeked around the corner at her sister, the gurgling machine, the swirling green fog. "Okay. But it doesn't seem right . . . leaving Dora and Mabel all hooked up like that."

"They're bewitched, Dez. You don't know what they could do."

She pulled the jackknife out of her pocket and snapped it open. Then she started toward the door.

I grabbed her arm again. "Wait . . . cover your mouth with your shirt, so you don't breathe the potion."

We both pulled our sleeves up over our hands and held the cloth to our mouths and noses. The minute we stepped into sight, all three girls went taut in their chairs. They glared at us through the steamy windows in their hoods. Mabel let out an ear-piercing yell and began thrashing in her chair. Luckily, Agnes and Serena had strapped her down good. She shook and struggled with such ferocity that I thought she'd bust the chair to pieces. Hoses snapped loose from her hood and green fog streamed into the room. The toads at the foot of her chair sprang up from their stupor and hopped in all directions, squealing and snapping.

Dez slashed through the straps around Clara's ankles, then the ones at her wrists. I lifted the hose-cluttered bonnet from her head, and a green cloud billowed out. I clamped my sleeve tight over my face, trying to hold my breath.

Clara smiled merrily up at Dez and me. She looked even prettier than before . . . in a strange sort of way. Her eyes were such a bright blue, they seemed to glow, and her hair had an orange shimmer. It danced around her head in perfect curls, almost like a crown.

"Let's go, Clara!" said Dez, gagging through her shirt sleeve. She yanked her sister out of the chair.

Clara stumbled to her feet, let out a hiccup, then gazed absently around the room, giggling.

"We've got to go!" I shouted. I couldn't hold my breath much longer. Fumes from the potion burned inside my nose.

Dez shoved her toward the storage room, but Clara shook loose and raced toward a table on the other side of the potion machine. She snatched her big canary hat off the table and put it on her head. It immediately rose into the air. She pulled it back down, giggling crazily, and tied the bow under her chin.

Then she scooped up a pair of scissors—a very large pair of scissors—and turned to Dez and me with a terrifying smile.

"Clara!" snapped Dez. "Put those down! It's time to go!"

Clara danced, twirling like a ballerina and snipping at the air with the scissors, toward Dora, who sat serenely beneath the gurgling contraption. Before we could stop her, Clara reached down and cut the strap from her friend's wrist. Dora yanked the hood from her head, and a gassy green cloud rolled down over her shoulders. I'd forgotten how gigantic she was—the size of a bear. She glowed like the sun, sitting there in her enormous yellow dress. Her hair was a mountain of golden ringlets. She tilted her head and gave me a puzzled look, her eyes glassy and distant, same as Clara's.

Lightning quick, her free hand shot out and grabbed my throat.

My lungs screamed for air. I pried at her fingers, helplessly. My head felt like it was going to burst.

Dez let out a holler and lashed at Dora's arm with a razor strap.

Clara giggled and spun with the scissors, humming to herself. She tried to cut the strap holding Dora's other arm, but Dez shoved her away. This whole time, Mabel had been lurching and struggling like a crazed beast. Leaping toads filled the air. Their shrieks rang in my ears as Dora's giant fingers clamped tighter around my throat . . . tighter, tighter, tighter . . .

My eyes went blurry . . . dizziness . . . darkness . . .

A steely *CLANG!* shook the room.

A gush of air filled my lungs and I crumpled to the floor.

Gazing up in a haze, I saw Dez with a cast-iron pot standing over Dora's slumped body. She dropped her weapon and helped me to my feet.

Mabel had gone quiet for a moment. She suddenly came to life again, rocking her chair with fresh fury. She kicked off from the floor with both feet, sending her chair over backward–pulling the entire potion machine down with her. Hoses and stovepipe burst apart, and the room filled with rolling green fog.

Mabel lay beneath the jumble, her chair smashed to kindling. She tore the hood from her head and glared up at us with a murderous leer.

"Dez!" I screamed.

She didn't argue this time. She grabbed hold of my arm, and we raced for the door.

17

Revenge of the Toad Witch

I HAD NEVER STARTED UP A TRUCK BEFORE, BUT I'd seen the Plinkett boys do it plenty of times. When Dez jumped into the driver's seat, I went straight to the front and set to turning the starter crank. The green fog in the beauty shop had left me bleary eyed and wobbly. It was a good thing we'd kept our mouths and noses covered, or we might've ended up like the witching maids.

"Pull out the throttle knob!" I hollered.

"What's it look like?" Dez hollered back.

It occurred to me that she had never driven a truck, either. We were in deep trouble.

A fury of crashing sounds came from inside the Magic Snippers—I could picture Dora smashing herself free of her chair. All three witching maids would be coming after us in a matter of seconds.

I ran around to the driver's door and yanked on the throttle knob, then raced to the front again and gave the crank a turn. The motor belched to a start. I jumped in next to Dez.

"Are you sure you know how to drive?" I asked, glancing back at the Snippers' doorway.

"Of course I do," said Dez in a rankled tone. "I watched Clara loads of times."

She kicked at the gas and break pedals like she was trying to stomp out a fire. She gave the shifting stick a tug, and the truck lurched backward. We slammed into the dead butternut tree with a jarring *CRUNCH!*

"Ar-ar-arooooooo!" The hunchback wolf let out a howl from somewhere across the barnyard.

Could things get any worse? Now Grobbs would be headed after us, too.

Dez kicked and pushed at every knob and pedal she could see, trying to get that truck to go frontways. Just then, the Snippers' door burst open, and the three witching maids stormed out with brooms in their hands. They ran toward us, shrieking.

I grabbed hold of the shifting lever and tugged it hard— just like I'd seen in the *Hodgeworth's Encyclopedia* diagram. Then I pushed down on Dez's knee, forcing her foot to stomp on the gas pedal. The truck heaved forward with an awful grinding sound.

Dez let out an excited hoot, and away we went. Dust and gravel sprayed up from the wheels. It rained down on the witching maids like scattershot.

"Watch out!" I hollered to Dez.

We were headed straight for my aunts' Franklin.

She gave the steering wheel a sharp yank, but too late. The truck raked across the side of the Franklin, and the sound of crunching metal filled the air. We scraped down the length of my aunts' car, snapping off pieces of both cars as we went. Then we veered off and plowed through a patch of dead sunflowers.

I held tight to my seat as Dez wheeled around the barnyard, dirt flying, smoke billowing, weeds whirling behind us. She could only seem to make the car turn right.

The witching maids straddled their broomsticks and began jumping up and down, as if trying to take off. We roared around them in a cloud of black smoke and dust. Then, against all laws of science and common sense, Dora's broom slowly lifted into the air. She rose ten feet, maybe more, wobbling and jerking, her enormous body perched impossibly on top of the spindly broom. She steadied herself and gazed down at me triumphantly. Then the broom went nose-up and she tumbled over backward. She dropped through the air and landed on top of Clara, and they both went down in a howling heap.

"Head for the Marsh Road!" I shouted.

"I'm trying!" Dez screamed back.

"Ar-ar-arooooo!" howled the wolf.

I let go of my seat and reached in front of Dez to turn on the headlights. Then I grabbed hold of the steering wheel and pointed us toward the marsh.

"Let go!" snapped Dez. "You'll make us crash!"

The truck bounced down the hill, spitting sand and

gravel. At the bottom, we plunged into the dip, sending up a shower of mud. The road stretched out in front of us, pocked with puddles and the stumps of chopped-off Strangle Oaks.

"We made it!" crowed Dez.

"Careful!" I reached over and yanked the steering wheel to the left just in time to dodge a stump.

The truck weaved back and forth across the road a few times, then straightened out. Dez leaned close to the dash and fixed her eyes on the track. I sat perched on the edge of my seat, ready to grab the steering wheel if necessary.

The Strangle Oaks were coming in fast now. They were sprouting up from the muddy road so thick I could barely see the track. In another hour, they'd be as high as the windshield. They let out a ghastly hissing sound as the truck barreled over them.

"Poor Clara." Dez choked back tears. "What if she's stuck that way . . . forever?"

"Careful," I said. "Keep your eyes on the road."

"Why would they do that?" She slammed the steering wheel with her fist. "Why would they bewitch somebody to be so mean and crazy?"

I checked out the back window to make sure we weren't being followed. "I don't think they meant for Clara to come out like that."

Dez wrinkled up her face.

"Think about it," I said. "Every time my aunts try to do a spell, or use a potion, it comes out wrong. Agnes tried to conjure open that busted door . . . and it turned into a man-eating tree thing. The Lullabeetle Silk . . . the Hornpout Powder . . . all of it came out different from what my aunts wanted. And every time, they blamed it on *the curse.*"

"What about the Howling Moonbeast Tonic?" said Dez, dodging a big pothole in the nick of time. "That sure seemed to work just dandy on Grobbs's wolf . . . or whatever that thing is."

She had a point there. I pondered for a minute, with one hand on the dashboard in close proximity to the steering wheel.

"I wonder . . ." I said. "Remember that creepy little man I told you about? Cousin Japeth? The back of his Packard was crammed to the brim with witching stuff. He told Serena it all came from their *friends overseas.* Made a big point of it."

Dez turned and gaped at me. "Other witches!"

I grabbed the wheel until she looked toward the road again. "I bet Agnes and Serena can only use potions that somebody else has mixed. Anytime they try to do magic themselves, it gets messed up. All they've got to do is touch the stuff and it's ruined."

Dez nodded pensively. "On account of the curse."

"That's why they needed witching maids," I went on. "To mix their potions and do their conjuring . . . for whatever it is they're trying to do. But because of the curse, they couldn't even get the witching maids to come out right. Not yet anyway."

Dez leaned back and sighed. "Poor Clara."

The truck splashed through a deep puddle and a blast of muddy water exploded across the windshield.

"Aw, darn it!" said Dez.

She took her golf hat off and reached around the windshield to clear a hole in the mud splatter.

"Here . . . let me." I pulled down my shirtsleeve and leaned out the window. "You mind the road."

I'd barely started wiping when something heavy slammed into the passenger door, lifting the truck up on two wheels. The blow knocked me back inside the cab, sprawled across Dez's lap.

"What was that?" Dez craned around to look behind us.

"Watch where you're going!" I shouted.

SLAM!

This time the thing hit the roof, leaving a crater-sized dent directly over my head. What in Sam Hill could fall from the sky and leave such a mark?

THUMP!

The jolt came from behind this time.

"Something's trying to knock us into the marsh!" I cried.

I scooted up close to Dez, away from the window, and peered out through the windshield. There was nothing out there—nothing but the swaying Strangle Oaks and a burnt-orange moon.

And then I saw it.

A dark blob tumbled through the sky, wobbling and swerving in the moonlight. The thing plunged into the treetops, then out again and across the marsh, barreling toward us through the cattails like a charging bull. I opened my mouth to holler, but no sound came out.

The dark shape burst out of the swamp grass just ahead of us and jerked to a stop in midair, right in the middle of the road.

Mabel the witching maid.

She sat on top of her broomstick, fierce eyed and grinning, toads crawling over her shoulders and legs. We barreled straight toward her.

"Look out!" I shouted.

Mabel's smile turned to panic as the truck slammed into her. There was a gruesome *THUMP* and a shriek as she rolled up over the windshield and disappeared. A couple of toads stuck to the glass.

I spun around and watched the road behind us—there was no sign of her.

But then I heard a noise above my head. Scuffling. Scraping. She was on the roof!

An arm swung in through the window and powerful fingers grabbed hold of my hair, nearly wrenching me out the door. Mabel leered in through the window upside down, licking her lips fiendishly. A half dozen toads tumbled into the cab.

"She's got me!" I dug my nails into the back of my seat with one hand and clawed at Mabel's fingers with the other.

"Hold on!" Dez swerved the truck back and forth across the lane, mud and water flying.

The Witches of Dredmoore Hollow

I was losing my hold on the seat, slipping farther and farther out the window. Mabel's breath was hot on my face. She was too strong—my grip gave way.

Dez gave the steering wheel a furious jerk. The truck lurched crazily, one wheel slamming hard into a pothole. With a howl, Mabel went tumbling off the roof into the darkness. I fell back into my seat with a gasp of relief.

Then the truck sailed into the marsh with a resounding *SPLASH.*

18

The Cracked Cauldron

DEZ AND I SPLASHED AND WALLOWED TOWARD shore. We took turns pulling each other out of holes and weed-tangles, and somehow we made it back to dry ground. The truck let out a watery burp and sunk into the black pool.

We lay there on the track a while, caked in mud, spitting out mouthfuls of pond silt. Pickerel grass clung to our hair.

We'd barely squeezed the water out of our shirtsleeves when the growl of a motor sounded across the swamp. Off in the distance, Grobbs's flatbed truck thundered down the hill toward the marsh. My aunts' Franklin bounced along behind him like a one-eyed beast–one headlight smashed to bits by Dez's wildcat driving.

I snatched hold of Dez's arm and pulled her into the cattails. We huddled behind a rotten stump, ankle deep in muck water. The truck and the Franklin rumbled toward us, heaving side to side down the track like bloodhounds sniffing for a scent. Agnes held a lantern out the window, studying the track as they went. Dez and I sunk down into the weeds, clinging tight to each other. As soon as their taillights disappeared into the mist, we slogged our way back to the road, shivering and miserable.

My eyes went longingly to the faraway light on my aunts' porch. Everywhere else was blind darkness.

"We better head back and find a place to hide," I said. "It's too dangerous out here on foot."

"No . . . we've got to keep going." Dez pulled the magic quill from beneath her hat and checked it over for damage. "We need to get help for Clara."

"But—"

"They'll give up searching for us after a while." She tucked the quill back under her golf cap. "We can run all the way to Blossom Springs in a few hours."

I shook my head, teeth chattering violently. "The Strangle Oaks . . . they'll cover the road in no time."

They'd grown a couple feet just in the last ten minutes. They were already as tall as cornstalks.

"These little things?" said Dez. "They aren't going to bother us any." She reached out and grabbed hold of a leaf.

Spindly branches wrapped around her wrist as if she'd sprung a trap. She screamed and pulled away. The leaves snapped free of the branch, clinging to her hand like a swarm of leeches.

"Get 'em off! Get 'em off!"

She slapped at her arms, trying not to touch the slimy

things with her fingers. I snatched a stick up off the ground and used it like a trowel to peel the leaves off her skin. They dropped to the ground and burrowed into the mud before you could blink. The Strangle Oak she'd touched let out a snaky hissing sound. The noise spread from tree to tree till every oak in the marsh shivered and hissed, filling the air with a beastly buzz.

Dez glanced around nervously, scratching at her arms as if they were still smothered with Strangle Oak leaves.

"Um . . . maybe you're right," she said.

"We can hide in the barn. Grobbs goes out to clear the Strangle Oaks off the road every morning. Soon as he's done, we can make a getaway."

She didn't argue this time. We set off running, doing our best to dodge the menacing oaks, our eyes fixed on my aunts' bobbing porch light.

I was breathless and wheezing by the time we bounded up the hill and into the barnyard. I never thought I'd be happy to see that rickety old house again–but I surely was.

So far, there'd been no further sign of Grobbs's truck or my aunts' Franklin. I knew they might come motoring back any second, though, so we headed for the backside of the barn. We intended to stay as far as possible from the Magic Snippers and those three witching maids. We clambered up onto the tin roof of the stable and snuck inside through a set of Dutch doors that led to the barn's upper floor. We hunkered behind a smelly horse trough, perking our ears for any sound. Then we buried ourselves in the nearest pile of straw, both of us worn out, cold, and shaking. Dez and I curled up together as snug as we could, too frozen and miserable to worry about whether it looked proper. Slowly the shivers wore off, and the hay warmed us up, and we drifted into a deep slumber.

There is no worse omen in all the world than being woken by the hoot of an owl. At least, that's what Grandma Ester told me once. And that's the first thing that came to my mind when I woke the next morning to a throaty cry–

Hoo! Hoo!

I lay still for a moment under the prickly hay, trying to recollect where I was. Dez's cheek lay against my shoulder, sprigs of straw poking out of her hair. Sunlight streamed down through a hole in the barn roof. We'd overslept. Grobbs would've cleared the road by now, and Agnes and Serena were probably up and about. I dug my way out of the hay pile and swept myself off.

"Dez!" I hissed, giving her a shake. "Wake up! We've got to–"

She sat up with a shout and planted a sharp punch on my jaw. I toppled backward, stars reeling overhead.

She sprang up from the hay, fists raised and ready to scrap. Finally she noticed me, sprawled out on the planks, rubbing my cheek.

"Oops. Sorry about that."

She helped me up. "You shouldn't go sneaking up on folks in their sleep."

"Thanks. I'll make a note of that." I wiggled my jaw—nothing seemed to be broken. "The sun's been up for hours. Agnes and Serena might already be at the Snippers."

Dez wasn't listening. Her eyes were fixed on something across the room. I turned to see a big stone table in the middle of the floor. On top of it sat a great black pot, big enough to cook a full-grown hog. It was busted up pretty badly—broken into several pieces, all held together with wooden braces and bailing twine.

Dez ran up to the table and circled the giant pot, flapping her hands with excitement. "Jumpin' jackrabbits! You know what this is? It's a *witching kettle!*"

A strange feeling stole over me. There was something familiar about the pot, though I'd never seen anything like it before. Danger and power radiated from the thing.

"It's a . . . witching cauldron," I said.

Everything in the room seemed to center around the enormous pot. Tables stacked with old books and papers; tins and jars full of witching sundries; the withered corpses of frogs, mice, and critters unknown. The floor was smattered with burnt twigs and ashes. I edged closer, scared and fascinated both at once.

There was a large mark on the cauldron, half hidden under bailing twine. I pushed the rope aside, revealing a rusty emblem:

$$\mathfrak{D}$$

All at once it struck me what I was looking at.

The night Grobbs had come to the Dredmoore family graveyard, he'd dug up five great clanking slabs—each about the size of these broken cauldron pieces. I remembered the words on the map I'd found at the dump wagon: *find all 5 pieces cast iron . . . beware of Burrowing Ravenweed . . .*

Agnes and Serena must've wanted that busted-up cauldron awfully bad to go to so much trouble. Grobbs, too, for that matter. But why had it been smashed up and buried in the Dredmoore graveyard in the first place?

As for the mark on the side—that was obvious enough: *D* for Dredmoore.

I tugged on Dez's elbow. "Grobbs must've cleared out the Strangle Oaks by now."

Slowly, I backed away from the cauldron—my eyes locked on its rusty, mysterious bulk. The back of my legs smacked into something solid and my feet shot out from under me. I sprawled on the floor next to a rickety wooden cage.

"Hoo-hoo!"

Two emerald eyes peered out through the bars.

Dez dropped to her knees and let out a whistle. A raggedy little barn owl hobbled out of the shadows and gazed back at her. The bird had the most unusual eyes I'd ever seen. They glowed like tiny green lanterns.

Dez wrenched the cage door open, and the owl hopped out onto the floor. A furry striped tail trailed behind it.

"He's got a *raccoon* tail!" cried Dez.

She studied the strange creature, leaning in close to see

whether the tail was real or not. Carefully, she reached down and ran her fingers along the length of the fur.

"*Hoo!*" The coon owl–or whatever it was–peered up at her, pleading with its round green eyes.

"Agnes and Serena must've tried to bewitch him," I guessed, "and he came out like that because of the curse."

"I bet they're fattening him up for one of their witch brews, poor fella." She pulled a rag from her pocket, took out a mangled biscuit, and sprinkled some crumbs on the floor. The creature lunged at the morsels and gobbled them down.

"He's nearly starved to death!" said Dez. "Aren't you, little man?"

"Why don't you leave him the rest of that biscuit?" I said. "We have to get moving."

"What about *him*?" She bent down and let the creature hop up onto her shirt sleeve. "We can't just leave him here to get boiled in some potion!"

She held out another handful of biscuit crumbs, which he gobbled up violently.

"I'm going to call him Mooneyes."

"He can take care of himself," I said, growing more impatient by the second. "He's got wings."

"I wonder . . ." Dez said. "Can you fly, Mooneyes? Even with that big ol' raccoon tail?"

She held up her arm with the strange beast perched on her wrist. "Go ahead, Mooneyes! You can do it!"

He gawked back at her blankly. "*Hoo-hoo-hoo.*"

"Flap like this!" Dez waved her free hand in the air. "Flap, flap, flap!"

"Lord almighty, Dez! We don't have time–"

Suddenly, Mooneyes leaped from her arm with a determined hoot and rose into the air, his striped tail wagging behind him. He circled the room a couple times, wobbling clumsily, then plunged headfirst into a wooden barrel. A puff of white dust plumed into the air.

"Mooneyes!" Dez ran to the barrel.

I clapped my hands over my eyes and shook my head. "Would you just bring the darn thing with you?"

When I looked up again, something caught my eye near the barrel. Two willow sticks lay on top of an old sea chest– both with burn marks on the tip.

Witching sticks–I was sure of it!

I stepped toward them slowly, even though a voice in the back of my head shouted for me to stay away.

What would it feel like to hold one?

"Wow!" Dez bounded up to the sea chest. Mooneyes perched on her shoulder, caked in white powder.

She grabbed the longer stick off the chest and lifted it into the air. She gave it a swish and shouted, "Heggledy peg!"

A tiny puff of smoke spurted from the end of the stick, and Dez choked back a surprised shout. "It's just like the witching stick Agnes used to conjure the door!"

"Hoo-hoo," said Mooneyes.

"You better put it back," I said hoarsely. "You don't know what it could do."

"Crackerjack!" shouted Dez. She gave the stick a snap, as if it was a horsewhip.

There was a sorry little sputter and another wisp of smoke. She frowned, pinching the end of the stick to see if it was hot.

"Hmm . . ." She held the stick up to my nose. "You give it a try."

I backed away, slamming into a table. "I really don't–"

"Aw, come on! If we can get it to shoot sparks or something, we can show it to the police."

"If it didn't work for you, why would it–"

Dez grabbed my wrist and slapped the witching stick into my hand.

I stood there a moment, half expecting the thing to blast to pieces in my fingers. I took a breath. Could I *feel* something? A quivering, buzzing sensation? Maybe it was just my own nerves. I had an overpowering urge to throw the thing on the floor and run.

But at the same time, I wondered . . .

What if I could make it . . . *do* something?

Surely, it couldn't hurt to try . . .

I raised the witching stick and tried to remember what Agnes had said to conjure the door. Instantly, a word popped into my head. It was a ridiculous, made-up word that I'd never even heard before. But out it came, rolling off my tongue before I had time to think about it. I snapped the witching stick forward as I shouted–

"Blunderblast!"

What happened next was a jumble. I felt the stick blast apart in my hands. The force of the blow sent me sprawling on the floor. High above me, a small, dark shape punched a hole in the barn roof and dropped from the sky like a comet. Then another . . . and another . . . smashing through the roof like oversized hailstones. Odd-shaped things . . . smoking and spinning as they fell. It took me a second to realize that they were *boots*.

Hot smoldering boots falling from the sky!

There was a stink of sulfur and burnt leather.

We most likely would've been pummeled unconscious if we hadn't scrambled under the stone table, Mooneyes clinging to Dez's collar. We crouched there, watching in wonder until the storm was over.

Smoldering boots covered the floor. Some of them twitched a few times, like dying fish. Then they let off a puff of black smoke and went still.

"Hot dandy!" Dez sprang out from beneath the table.

I gawped at the floor, my heart beating away like mad. Had *I* done this? The scorched boots. The exploded witching stick. Smoke winnowing from the mess.

The back of my hand was flecked with burns. There was a red line across my palm where I'd been singed by the willow.

Dez snatched the other stick off the chest and raised it into the air.

"Don't!" I covered my head.

She clenched her teeth and shouted–

"Blunderblast!"

The stick made a sputtering noise, and a tiny belch of smoke coughed from the end.

She looked at the tip of the stick and scowled. Then she drew back her arm and tried it again. Nothing. She kept at it for a few minutes, shouting louder every time, but all she managed to do was shake Mooneyes off her shoulder.

"This one must be busted. You give it a try."

She shoved the stick into my hand just as a loud *click* rang across the room—the sound of a door latch snapping open.

19

～⊶⊷～

Snout Stones

I STUFFED THE WITCHING STICK INTO THE BACK of my trousers and tugged Dez behind a stack of hay bales, Mooneyes clutching on to her shoulder again. My aunts' voices boomed up into the room.

"Even if we find the boy, what good will it do?" said Agnes. "The Bristle Sprout Tonic won't be much use on a drowned corpse. The only Dredmoore boy since the curse, and he's gone. We'll be stuck like this forever . . . with these backwoods bumpkin girls to do our witching for us."

"What makes you so certain the boy is dead, Sister?" said Serena.

I heard the trapdoor in the floor pop open and then slam shut. Footsteps clattered to the middle of the room and stopped. The sisters went silent. I peeked around the side of the haystack and saw them taking in the sight of all those burnt boots I'd conjured down from the sky and the barn roof peppered full of holes.

"Did you let the witching maids in here yesterday?" Serena asked sharply.

"No, 'course not," said Agnes.

"Then where'd this mess come from? There's got to be a thousand boots on the floor. Someone had to conjure them."

"That one with the toads has gotten pretty clever," Agnes suggested. "Maybe she got hold of a witching stick–"

"Those witching sticks I left on the chest–they're gone, too!" cried Serena. "Are you sure you locked up yesterday?"

"The boy!" cried Agnes. "He must've snuck in here and took those witching sticks yesterday . . . just before he ran off in that jalopy."

I could hear them digging around to see what else was missing. The witching stick in the back of my trousers let out a fierce swell of heat. I wanted to toss the thing, get it as far away from me as I could. Footsteps clip-clopped toward our hiding spot behind the hay bales.

There was a raggedy blanket draped over a big pile of something or other off in one corner. I signaled for Dez to follow, and we crawled on hands and knees across the floor. Mooneyes hopped down from Dez's shoulder and skittered after us. We ducked under the blanket. There was a hollow between a pair of big, lumpy rocks. I felt around and found a place to sit, tucked up against one of the stones. I pawed it over and realized it was a statue. It seemed to be half sitting, half lying down. I could make out the shape of a chest, shoulders, and legs. A granite arm pointed into the air just above my head, holding up the blanket.

"Well, no matter about the witching sticks," said Serena. "If the boy has them, we'll get them back soon enough. If not, we've still got that boxful that Japeth and the twins brought back from overseas. Anyhow . . . we may as well get started on the Mending Brew."

"Mending Brew?" Agnes snorted. "How do you plan to do that without the boy? Grobbs says he drowned in the marsh. The wolf would've sniffed him out otherwise."

"Goodness, Sister," Serena said with a chuckle. "I didn't know you put such stock in Mr. Grobbs."

"Why would he lie? He wants that boy caught as much as we do."

"I know thinking is not your strong suit," said Serena. "But sometimes I worry about you, Agnes dear. I truly do. Virgil Grobbs only follows orders to keep his precious wolf alive. The witching maids have been *potioned* to obey. They'll do exactly as they're told—with no second thoughts about it. And now they've got better tracking noses than the wolf."

"What do you mean, *tracking noses*?"

"I gave them each a Snout Stone, of course," said Serena. "Cousin Japeth left us a half dozen."

"Then the witching maids are out in the swamp . . . tracking the boy?"

"That's right, Sister. They'd be back by now if he'd drowned. Snout Stones don't lie. They should be catching up with our nephew any minute now."

Dez clutched on to my arm. No doubt she was thinking the same thing I was: *would the witching maids be able to follow my scent to the barn?*

"Now stop your fretting and fetch me some Scab Root," said Serena.

I found a hole in the blanket and peeked out just as Agnes yanked a withered shrub down from a ceiling rafter.

All this time, Mooneyes had never made a peep, perched there on Dez's lap. He pecked lazily at her bootlaces, his green eyes glowing eerily. Suddenly, he jumped up and aimed a nip at Dez's pocket.

"*Ow!*" she hollered without thinking.

"*Hoo!*" screeched Mooneyes, leaping into the air.

Wings, claws, and raccoon tail filled the space of our tiny hideaway.

"What was that?" croaked Agnes.

I dug into Dez's pocket, pulled out the rag full of biscuit crumbs, and tossed them out from under the blanket.

"*Hoo-hoo!*" Mooneyes sprang after the crumbs.

I clamped my hand over Dez's mouth. Footsteps clattered over next to our hiding spot. I held my breath.

"Oh, it's only that barn owl that the witching maids used for practice," said Agnes. "Must've gotten out of his cage."

My heart felt like thunder in my chest as I watched two pairs of shoes step up to the edge of the blanket.

"You must've left the latch open," said Serena.

"I most certainly did not," Agnes huffed. "I clearly

recall locking that cage shut."

"No need to get your hackles up," said Serena. "We all make mistakes now and again."

"Oh! Of course it *had* to be me! Couldn't have been Grobbs or the witching maids? You think I'm so entirely useless–"

Agnes was interrupted by a great commotion from across the room. The trapdoor burst open again, and a furious trample of feet raced toward us. A foul stench filled the air, along with a beastly snorting noise that sounded like a herd of wild hogs.

Without warning, the blanket flew from our heads. Serena and Agnes stared down at us in surprise. In front of them stood the three witching maids, crazy eyed and panting, Mabel surrounded by her swarm of toads. Each of the girls held a dirty pink stone shaped like a pig snout. The stones jerked madly in their hands, sniffing at the air. All three witching maids lunged toward me, shrieking. Before I could move, I was buried in a whirlwind of Snout Stones, groping fingers, and pouncing toads.

Agnes drove the witching maids away with her parasol.

Serena fought back a smile as she took in the situation. "Seems our nephew has found himself a girlfriend."

Her fox wrap let out a snicker.

Agnes knocked off Dez's golf cap with the tip of her parasol. "Are you sure it's a girl?"

Dez clenched her fists and sprang to her feet–or at least that's what she meant to do. She'd forgotten about the arm of the statue directly above her head. There was a horrible *thunk!* as she slammed her forehead into the stone elbow. She fell back to the floor, limp as a wet rope, blood welling up over her eyebrow. I put my arm around her as she cradled her head in her hands, moaning.

There was nowhere to run. The witching maids grinned down at us, the Snout Stones lurching in their hands.

"The boy must've heard everything we said," muttered Agnes.

Serena pursed her lips and nodded.

Dez glared up at Serena, rubbing her head. A trickle of blood ran down the side of her face. "You'll pay for what you've done to Clara." She nodded toward her sister, who was struggling to control the Snout Stone and keep her hat from drifting off at the same time.

My mind raced for a plan . . . a distraction . . . anything. . . . The witching stick in the back of my trousers gave off a surge of heat.

"My parents know what you're doing!" I shouted. "Dez sent them letters I wrote! They'll be here any minute!"

"That's right!" hollered Dez, catching on to my lie. "And we told 'em to bring every policeman in the county!"

My aunts looked at each other and burst into laughter.

"Well, I can't speak for the county police," said Serena. "But I'm afraid Elijah's folks won't be much help anytime soon."

The look in her eyes was so evil it nearly knocked me over. Agnes pointed her parasol, smirking wickedly, and

I turned to stare at the statue I'd been leaning against all this time.

It was Mama.

Her face was granite gray, her eyes and mouth open in horror. One hand was cocked back, like she was trying to swat something away. She was solid stone, from head to toe.

"Your pa's here, too," said Agnes, tapping the tip of her parasol on the other statue.

Poppers lay serenely in his nightshirt, fast asleep. He was curled up tight against a stone pillow.

"What . . . what did you do to them?" My voice sounded distant, as if someone else was speaking. I couldn't breathe.

Did this mean they were dead?

"Tomb Creeper poison." Agnes curled her fingers into the shape of a spider. "Gruesome creature. Painful bite. Must've been awful."

I looked up at Mama's horrified face, heartsick. "Why . . . ? Why would you–"

"Believe me, Elijah," said Serena sweetly, "we didn't want to go to such . . . unpleasant measures." The delight in her eyes told me different. "We had no choice. We had to get them out of the way so we could get what we needed . . . from you."

"I don't know what you're talking about! I don't have anything you could want. I've got nothing!" Tears streamed down my face as I held up my empty hands, shaking, powerless. . . .

"Hush, nephew . . . hush . . ." Serena reached down and wiped the tears from my cheek with the back of her glove. The fox wrap scrunched its face up into a mocking pout. "You're right. You don't have anything we want . . . yet."

Agnes stuck the tip of her parasol under my chin, her purple eyes gleaming. "But you will soon."

20

Curse Be Broken, Curse Be Spurned

IT GRIEVED ME SOMETHING AWFUL TO THINK that Mama and Poppers had been stuck like that for so long. I'd sat around waiting, mad at them for running off and leaving me with Agnes and Serena—and the whole while, they'd been worse off than me.

I still didn't know what it meant for them to be turned to stone, whether they were dead or alive. Could my aunts conjure them back to life again? Back to the way they were? The sneer on Agnes's face—gloating and victorious—told me they had other plans.

They trussed up Dez and me to a barn beam near the broken cauldron, while they fluttered around the place, fetching ingredients and hollering orders at the witching maids, who jumped at every command.

Dez was a frightful sight—a swollen gash on her forehead and blood crusted down the side of her face. But she hardly seemed to notice. She gnawed at the ropes around her wrists in a wildcat fury. That girl was fierce to the end, no question about it.

Mooneyes hooted mournfully from his cage across the room where Agnes had locked him up again. His green eyes were fixed on Dez with a forlorn expression.

Still, no matter how bleak it all appeared, I knew I needed to keep thinking . . . to keep trying to figure a way out of this. I told myself that Mama and Poppers were going to be all right. There had to be a way to get them back to normal. There just had to be. But the more I thought about it, the more worked up and scared I got—and the witching stick grew hotter and hotter against the skin on my back.

Agnes stepped away from the witching maids' foul-smelling concoctions and slithered up to me.

"Ropes aren't too tight, I hope?" She gave the ends a sharp tug, cinching them even tighter.

Dez stopped working at her knots. She spat a mouthful of chewed-up rope at Agnes. "You'll be sorry! Won't be long before folks'll come looking for Clara and me! You'll have the whole town of Blossom Springs to reckon with!"

Agnes ignored Dez and followed my gaze across the room to the statues of Mama and Poppers. "I wouldn't worry too much about your mama. She can't feel any pain. Nor anything else for that matter."

A deep bitterness shone in her eyes. I glared back at her in hateful silence.

"The Tomb Creeper poison was Serena's idea," she said sourly. "Things wouldn't have gone so gentle if I'd had my way. Your mama deserved worse–much worse. All those years we suffered on account of what she did . . . to the whole Dredmoore family. But I guess you don't know about that. It was your mama that put the curse on the cauldron."

Her eyes lit up at the confusion on my face.

"Oh, there's a great many things your mama never told you! So high and mighty–her and your grandma Ester! They didn't like the way some of us used our . . . *abilities*. We had plans for the cauldron, a few of us did. We weren't afraid to take what it could offer. One of us would've been the Keeper, Serena or me. Would've controlled the cauldron . . . controlled everything. It would've been perfect. But Katrina . . . she and Grandma Ester decided the Dredmoore gift was too powerful . . . too dangerous for anyone to use . . . even themselves. So your mama searched till she found a way to put a stop to it all. The Blighted Broomstick Curse it was called. Shattered the cauldron to pieces, and all the Dredmoore powers along with it. Ruined everything! Not a thing we could do . . . not any of us! Witching sticks burst apart in our hands. We had no control over our conjuring. Whatever we touched–tonics, potions, charms–it all came out muddled and useless."

She paused a moment, staring down at the floor, lost in her spiteful thoughts. Then she looked up and saw the horror in my eyes . . . the confusion . . . the seething anger.

She held the tip of her parasol to my chest, her eyes alight with cruel joy. "Never told you a word of this, did she?

You never had the slightest notion whatsoever that your mama was a *witch*."

The blood rushed from my head. The whole world went blurry.

It was a lie. A lie!

Mama would never . . . It just wasn't possible . . .

"You're lying!" I lunged at her, but the ropes jerked me back. "My mama's nothing like you! *Nothing!*"

Agnes shook her head. "Oh, you're right about that, Nephew. But she's got Dredmoore blood . . . so like it or not, she's got the gift. Same as your sweet old grandma Ester and the rest of the family." She leaned closer and hissed into my ear, "Same as *you!*"

My head pounded with noise, rage, bewilderment. Dez stared at me with a pained expression.

Mama, a witch? All these years . . . ?

And me? Me, too? The idea was impossible. Insane. If I had witching powers, wouldn't I know about it?

My mind searched for arguments . . . for proof that Agnes was lying. But a flurry of images flashed through my head: *strange lights and sounds in the Dredmoore grave-yard . . . the family of vicious ravens that only Mama could drive away . . . the willow switch she kept under her pillow for reasons I could never fathom . . . the packages from Dredmoore relations that she'd thrown into the woodstove, unopened . . . all the times Mrs. Plinkett had come to give me medicine instead of Mama her-self . . . a hundred little moments like these, odd happenings that I'd always thought of as nothing more than "Mama's ways" . . .*

Could she really have lied to me all this time? Could she truly have kept such a secret?

A puff of green smoke rose from the corner of the room where Serena and the witching maids had been laboring. Mabel let out a raspy whoop, and a flurry of toads sprang up all around her. She lifted a steaming stone bowl and leered over at me. Clara and Dora clapped their hands, and broke into a promenade around the cauldron.

"My goodness, Sister!" said Serena, walking toward us. "Whatever did you say to our nephew to put him in such a state of despair?"

"I figured he ought to know the truth." Agnes eyed the bowl in Mabel's hands greedily. "How his mama left the entire Dredmoore family in ruin."

"It's a lie!" I cried weakly.

"The boy's right, you know." Serena gestured Mabel toward a shelf, where she set down the bowl of steaming goop. "Katrina did us a great favor."

Agnes gawped at her sister. "What in blazes—"

"It's true," Serena went on. "If Katrina hadn't used the curse, Mother would still be Keeper of the cauldron. She'd still have final say on all the conjuring. Wouldn't she?"

"I suppose that's one way to look at it," scoffed Agnes.

"No, dear, it's the *only* way," said Serena. "Now that the cauldron is broken, there's no Keeper. It has no master at all, and the Dredmoore gift is a shambles. But once it's mended! Ah! That will change everything, now, won't it? It will be the first dark magic Choosing in a hundred years!"

She put her hand against my cheek. "And we'll owe all of our thanks to mother and son. To Katrina for destroying the cauldron . . . and Elijah for *mending* it."

Serena directed the witching maids to clear off a table built from a splintered door. They strapped me down to it, splayed out on my back, and cinched my hands and feet as tight as they could. It was Dora's job to pin down my head. Her giant hands were so powerful I thought she'd crush my skull. The fox wrap gazed down at me from Serena's shoulder, smacking its withered lips.

"What are you going to do to him?" howled Dez, thrashing against her ropes. "Leave him alone!"

No one so much as turned to look at her. Not even Clara.

"Mabel, dear," said Serena, "is the Bristle Sprout Tonic ready?"

Mabel's bulging eyes lit up, and she nodded excitedly. She sniffed at the air, then bent over and snatched a beetle off the table with a flash of her tongue.

"No need to worry, Elijah," said Serena, turning to me with a wink. "In the past few days, the witching maids have become quite talented at conjuring . . . thanks to the Croneswort that Cousin Japeth brought us. No easy feat, mind you. Sister and I had our doubts for the longest time—what with all the witching sticks exploding, and everything turning into toadstools and maggots . . . and that awful business with the rat that turned inside out. But they've come along wonderfully, our little witching maids. Especially Mabel. Haven't you, my sweet?"

Mabel simpered, batting her enormous eyelashes. A toad wriggled out of her sleeve and made a tiny puddle on the table.

I was helpless as a snared rabbit. The room spun. Whatever it was they planned to do, why didn't they just get it over with?

Agnes reached for the stone bowl next to me, but Serena snatched her wrist in midair.

"Have you learned nothing, Sister?" Serena's face was red and twisted. "Do you insist on ruining *everything*?"

Agnes stepped back, staring at her own hand as if she'd never seen it before.

"I . . . I . . . don't know what came over me."

"The witching maids must do *all of it*," said Serena. "You and I must *touch* nothing, and *do* nothing."

Agnes nodded, her lip curled spitefully. She shrunk farther away from the table, drawing her parasol tight against her chest.

"All right, Mabel." Serena turned to her favorite witching maid with a motherly smile. "You know what to do, my sugar lump. Just as we practiced."

Mabel lifted the stone bowl again and shot a menacing glance at my throat.

"Please, Aunt Serena!" I strained against the ropes, my head going dark and dizzy.

Dora tightened her hold. I let out an agonized groan. Dez wrenched at her ropes, screaming, until Agnes jabbed her in the ribs with her parasol.

"Now, now, Elijah," whispered Serena. "Bristle Sprout Tonic is quite painless . . . unless Mabel gets carried away with those prickly little teeth of hers. But you won't do that, will you, Mabel?"

Mabel lifted the bowl to her plentiful lips and slurped. Black ooze dribbled down the corners of her mouth.

"Please!" I howled.

As soon as she'd drained the bowl, Mabel let out a ferocious belch and dropped the stone dish to the floor. Then she stepped toward me, oily black juice dripping from her lips. Toads sprang from her shoulders and hair, scrambling over my chest and legs. I shut my eyes, bracing myself for pain . . . for something dreadful . . .

A disgusting wet kiss pressed against my chin.

That was all.

Mabel stepped back, gurgling proudly. Toads swarmed from the table, disappearing into the nest of her hair and the billows of her dress.

"Well?" Agnes elbowed in between her sister and Mabel. "Did it work?"

"Patience, Sister." Serena squinted at my chin. Dora lifted her mammoth hands, letting the blood rush back into my head.

"What did you do to me?" My voice was barely a whisper. "Am I going to die?"

"Look!" cried Agnes. *"There it is! It's growing!"*

Serena leaned in toward my face and nodded with satisfaction. Her fox wrap rubbed its nose against her neck and cooed.

Dez stared at me from across the room, studying me for some mysterious change.

I drew my hand toward my face as best I could with the ropes around my wrists. It took all the strength I had, but finally, the tip of my finger touched the end of my jaw.

And then I felt it.

Poking out from the oily wet of Mabel's kiss was a single prickly whisker growing from my chin.

A foul stench rose from the cauldron, stinging my eyes and lungs. I coughed and gagged, tearing at my ropes.

Serena shouted orders at the witching maids as they tossed kindling on the fire and filled the cauldron with ghastly ingredients: a spoonful of hornet stingers, a toenail from a one-legged man, fifty-three earwigs, a bottle of leech bile, and dozens of other such abominations. Dora stirred the reeking mess with a fat stick. Agnes gazed anxiously into the brew, clutching her parasol so tight that her knuckles went white. Dez hollered murderous threats from across the room as she yanked and gnawed at her ropes. And Mooneyes rattled his beak against the bars of his cage.

"The Mending Brew is ready," said Serena. She gestured to Mabel, who loomed over me, pinching at the air with a pair of rusty tweezers.

Mabel gave a little hop of joy and craned toward my face. Her lips were still smeared with black Bristle Sprout Tonic. I shook my head back and forth as violently as I could, but Dora grabbed hold of my ears. She whistled merrily as she clamped my head to the table again.

Clara stepped up on the other side of the table holding a small tin. She took off the lid and peered into it with a dazed expression.

"Be very, very careful, Mabel dear," said Serena. "Everything depends upon that whisker."

Mabel's eyes bulged even more than usual as she bore down on my chin in concentration. She held her breath. Her cheeks puffed out, blazing red.

The room went so quiet the only thing I could hear was Mooneyes' throaty moan—a sound of utter despair. I felt a quick sting as Mabel plucked the whisker from my chin. Then I heard the *clack* of the tweezers against the tin as she deposited the prize.

A sigh of relief swept over the room.

"Thank you, Elijah," said Serena, signaling for Dora to let go of me. "You can't possibly know what a generous thing you've done for Agnes and me. For the whole Dredmoore family, really."

She motioned for Mabel and Clara to continue with their preparations.

"We tried a great many things over the years, but the curse always got the best of us. You can see the muddle we were in—so long as the cauldron was broken, we had no control over our magic. And without magic, there was no way to mend the cauldron. Very clever of your mother, wasn't it?" She sighed and cast an affectionate glance over at Mama's statue in the corner.

"Took us years to track down a counter spell," Serena went on. "You'd think no one had ever broken a cauldron before. Then, once we found it, we had a new challenge to deal with. The Mending Brew was a simple recipe, for the most part—a bit of crow's foot, a couple moldy roots, the usual sort of thing. All but for one very important ingredient . . ."

Serena paused and widened her eyes, teasingly. "The first whisker from a boy of Dredmoore blood!"

She turned and gazed into the tin as Mabel held it up for her to inspect. "Isn't it marvelous? And no one but you could've provided it, Elijah."

Agnes thumped her parasol on the floor. "We've wasted enough time on the boy. It's time we get on with the mending."

Serena stepped back from the tin. "Right you are, Agnes! Your inclination to keep things on track should work in your favor at the Choosing Ceremony."

Agnes's face went crimson. "You and I both know better than that, Sister. You're the one that'll get chosen, so there's no need to be pert about it."

Serena directed the witching maids to gather around the cauldron. Mabel held the tin with my whisker, while Dora stirred and Clara fanned the fire. When Serena gave the signal, Mabel lifted the tin and tipped the whisker into the cauldron. A great mushroom of smoke rose from the brew, and the air crackled with energy.

The sisters glanced at each other and nodded. Their faces were grave and still. They raised their hands, closed their eyes, and began to chant:

Sting of hornet, tail of newt,
Bowel of leech and blighted root,
Pinch of hair, avenge the sin,
Manhood's shadow on the chin,
Curse be broken, curse be spurned,
Dredmoore powers be returned!

No sooner had they finished their chanting than the cauldron lit up in red. The ropes that held it together burst into flames and disappeared with a hiss. The cracks sealed shut—each with a thunderous *CLANG!*—and a spout of black smoke shot into the air.

A fierce wind rose from the cauldron. Agnes's and Serena's hair stood on end. Dim blue light sprayed from their fingertips. The air screamed with noise and heat, and the smell was wonderful and terrible all at once. I lay there strapped to the table, overcome with dizziness. My skin tingled. The whole room seemed to be spinning, caught up in the churning brew.

Something was happening to me. A feverish energy swept over me, instantly drenching me with sweat. The hairs on my arms went prickly. I thrashed wildly, ropes biting into my wrists and ankles. Every inch of my body sizzled with electricity.

Then, just as quickly as it had come, the feeling slipped away spilling out through my fingertips in a great rush. I went limp and fell back against the table, gasping for breath.

All at once I knew that the curse had been broken. The Dredmoore cauldron was mended. And I would never be the same again.

Part 3

Witches have been a colorful constituent in the folklore of nearly every culture throughout the ages. Modern science, however, has proven that the laws of nature alone govern the capabilities of the human race, and the subject of witches and witchery deserves no place in scholarly discourse.

—*Hodgeworth's Encyclopedia of Natural Science*

21

Tomb Creepers

IN THE CHILL OF NIGHTFALL, THE WITCHING maids untied Dez and me, and stuffed us into a big rusty cage. Then they hauled us outside. Porcupine quills stuck up from the floor of our prison, jabbing our hands and legs. It was clear by the odor that many an unfortunate creature had died and rotted in that cage. Dora hoisted us up onto the back of Grobbs's Ford. She hauled out the statues of Mama and Poppers and set them next to us. Then she lugged out the Dredmoore cauldron and heaved that onto the truck as well. It was still warm and foul smelling from the day's conjuring. Mabel, surrounded by the usual mob of toads, roped everything down to the truck bed, stopping now and then to poke at Dez and me with a busted broomstick.

Dez banged on the cage and pleaded with Clara to come help us, but her sister may as well have been deaf. She danced around the barnyard, leaping and twirling, singing like a deranged sparrow. Mooneyes hooted through an upstairs window in a grief-stricken tone, as if calling for Dez.

There was a great flurry of coming and going from the barn—my aunts were clearly preparing for some sort of journey. They were so giddy to have their witching powers back that they pointed their sticks at everything in sight. Lightning cracks and puffs of green smoke filled the air. Tree stumps exploded and clumps of sod flew all over the barnyard.

Serena floated a crate full of potion bottles out the barn window and set it on the backseat of the Franklin without so much as a rattle. When Agnes tried the same thing, her box plowed into a butternut tree, scattering petrified fish heads across the ground.

Dez let out a shrieking laugh and ducked down in our cage.

Agnes whirled around, her witching stick raised, her eyes smoldering.

Serena caught hold of her wrist. "Patience, Agnes dear. All you need is a little practice and your conjuring will be as good as before."

"*You* don't seem to be having any trouble." Agnes sniffed.

All this time, while Dez and I sat trapped in our cage, tiny jolts of heat kept stinging my bottom. The witching stick in the back of my trousers seemed intent on reminding me it was there. I hadn't forgotten. How could I? I'd felt a change course through my blood the moment the cauldron was mended . . . though I wasn't sure what it all meant. Could I just pull out the witching stick and use it to blast open the cage? For all I knew, I might blow Dez and myself to smithereens. Or, more likely, nothing would happen at all.

The stick nagged at me as I watched Agnes and Serena pack up Grobbs's truck and the Franklin. I didn't know where they planned to take us all, but now that they'd gotten what they needed, I had an uncomfortable hunch that our part in the plan was over.

"Why are we going to all this bother?" Agnes grumbled as she stuffed a pair of broomsticks into the car. "Why don't we hold the ceremony right here? Then the cauldron would just pick between you and me, and we'd have it done with."

"Agnes, dear, you have absolutely no conception of how the Choosing works, do you?" said Serena as she conjured a stack of books neatly onto the backseat.

"Well, how would I? There hasn't been one since before—"

"The ceremony requires at least *five* living Dredmoores—the cauldron was conjured to work that way from the start. To prevent any one person from . . . causing mischief, so to speak. I'm sure I've explained this all to you before."

"You don't need to be so—"

"And since this will be a *dark magic* Choosing, you'll need to learn the proper incantation. You don't recollect that, either? It truly is a wonder how you get through the day."

The fox wrap gave a wicked snicker.

"No matter," said Agnes bitterly. "You'll be the one that gets chosen."

"Now, now, Agnes. You don't know that for sure." Serena shut the Franklin's back door with a flick of her witching stick. "The cauldron might just as likely pick you."

By the tone of her voice, I could tell she didn't believe a word of it. She gave her sister a little pat on the shoulder. Then she headed toward the barn for another load of supplies. Agnes followed after her, jabbing her parasol hard into the ground with every step.

They'd barely gone out of sight when, from nowhere, Grobbs stepped up to the truck. He threw a dark look at Dez and me, then at the barn door. He leaned in close to the bars of our cage, his breath reeking of licorice root.

"You should've run off like I told you, boy!" he growled. "Now look what it's come to."

He pulled back his coat, and the moonlight twinkled off the silver head of a hatchet. I sunk back in the cage, pulling Dez along with me as she let out an ear-shattering scream.

"Hush, girl!" Grobbs stole another nervous glance at the barn.

Mooneyes burst into a hooting frenzy from his cage inside the barn, and Jack the wolf joined in with a throaty howl from a nearby nettle patch.

Grobbs was about to lift the hatchet out of its holster when the Snippers' door burst open and a huge wooden chest came drifting out into the yard. Serena padded calmly behind it, coaxing it through the air with her stick. Agnes and the witching maids trailed after her, swaying beneath overloaded boxes.

Grobbs let his coat fall back over the hatchet and pretended to tighten the knots holding our cage to the truck.

"Everything ready, Mr. Grobbs?" asked Serena. She twitched her stick a few times to tidy all the supplies she'd piled into the Franklin.

"All due respect, ma'am," he said, looking her square in the eyes, "I think it's time you settled your end of the deal. Once you've done that, I'll feel a whole lot better about finishing up our business."

Agnes drew her witching stick out of her parasol in a flash, her eyes blazing. Serena tapped her sister's wrist, gently, till Agnes lowered her arm. The fox wrap made a shushing sound.

"I always did like that about you, Mr. Grobbs," said Serena. "Always straight to the point."

"Yes'm," said Grobbs. "I like to know how things stand."

"As you should." Serena nodded solemnly. "You've held up your end of the bargain without fail. Goodness knows, not many would've had the fortitude to chop down those Strangle Oaks every day. Or to face that Burrowing Ravenweed." She glanced down at the stump on his left arm and gave her head a sorrowful shake. "Jack is lucky to have such a true friend. I know it was awfully difficult, waiting all this time. You certainly did your part to help us break the curse, so I don't see any reason we can't set poor Jack right again."

"I'd surely appreciate it, ma'am."

"Well, you've always been trustworthy, Mr. Grobbs. I'm confident that won't change once Jack is put back to his old self, will it?"

"No, ma'am."

Serena pulled off her gloves. "Why don't you call him over here, and let's see if we can put a shake in his tail again, hmm?"

Grobbs whistled for Jack. The wolf hoisted himself up out of the nettle patch and lurched across the grass toward the truck. Serena lifted the gold chain from around her neck and took the stopper from the tiny green bottle. She poured a drop of the Howling Moonbeast Tonic on the end of Jack's nose. Then she touched the top of his head with her witching stick and whispered some words I couldn't hear.

Jack let out a terrible yelp and threw himself down on the grass. He writhed on the ground, howling and snarling and kicking his legs in agony.

"It's killing him!" Grobbs reached for the wolf.

Serena took his arm. "Wait a minute . . . give it time."

Grobbs clenched his fist as Jack rolled back and forth on the ground. Thick clumps of fur flew every which way. His howls turned to whimpers. Then he stopped moving altogether.

"There," said Serena. "It's done."

She let go of Grobbs, and he dropped to the creature's side.

Jack sprang to his feet and shook. A cloud of hair flew all around him. He pounced, planting his front paws on his master's chest, and nearly bowled him over. Dez and I clung to the bars of our cage, dumbstruck.

It was miraculous. Jack was no longer the lumbering hunchbacked wolf I'd feared for so long. He'd changed into a floppy-eared hound dog, friendly and happy and bouncing with energy. Grobbs's face lit up with joy as Jack jumped all over him, licking his neck and ears.

"Thank you kindly, Mizz Dredmoore," said Grobbs.

I even thought I saw him wipe a tear from his cheek.

"The pleasure's entirely mine, Mr. Grobbs," said Serena. "Agnes and I are always good to our word. I'm sure we can trust the same of you?"

Grobbs looked up and gave her a single nod, his eyes grim and dangerous.

My aunts went back to their packing.

It was all up to me now. There was no way around it. Mama and Poppers were turned to stone, and who could guess what my aunts might've done with Grandma Ester? Soon Agnes and Serena would have the Franklin loaded. If Dez and I couldn't figure out some kind of escape, it might just be the end for all of us.

I glanced over at Dez. She was trying to saw through the bars of the cage with a rusty nail. She'd managed to wear a little groove in the metal, but she was likely to die of old age before she made it all the way through.

Like it or not, there was only one choice I could think of—and not the slightest reason to believe it would even work. I took a deep breath, building up the nerve. Then I tapped Dez on the shoulder and drew the witching stick from behind me.

Her eyes grew wide as silver dollars. I clapped my hand over her mouth.

"Shh!"

I pulled my hand away slowly.

She leaned in close to the stick and whispered, "But . . . where . . . ?"

"I hid it in the back of my trousers when we were in the barn."

Her face went red hot. "You mean you had that thing all this time and you never used it?"

I turned the witching stick over in my hands. A tiny tremor ran through it—or maybe it was just my imagination—sending a warm tingle up my arm. All of a sudden I wished I hadn't taken the stick out . . . hadn't showed it to Dez. Even if I tried to use it, I'd be no match for Agnes and Serena. I didn't know any conjure words—not real ones, anyhow. Last time I tried, all I'd managed was to make a bunch of boots fall out of the sky.

I could hear a faint sound coming from the stick—a low and eerie hum.

Dez grabbed my wrist excitedly and pointed the witching stick at the cage door. "Go ahead! Blast it open!"

I stared at the rusty bars, my mind gone fuzzy. "I . . . I don't know the conjure words."

"Just say whatever pops into your head! You can do it! You've got the Dredmoore gift, same as your aunts!"

No sooner had Dez spoken than Agnes and Serena stepped out of the Snippers' door, followed by Dora with an armful of broomsticks. Clara and Mabel sauntered along behind, each toting a load of books and papers.

"Here they come!" said Dez. "Smack the whole bunch of 'em with a fireball!"

I pulled away from her and stuffed the witching stick under my leg. She stared at me in disbelief.

Serena stepped up to the truck and looked me in the eyes with a deep sigh. "I truly do wish we'd met under different circumstances, Elijah. I think we'd have gotten along grandly, you and I. It grieves me more than I can say to have it end like this. Agnes and I are eternally beholden to you. We never could've broken the curse without your help."

"He didn't *help* you with nothing!" hollered Dez. "You did it all with foul rotten black magic! Foul and rotten like *you*!"

Serena tilted her head and gave Dez an amused smile. She drew her witching stick from beneath the fox wrap, then poked it through the bars of the cage and tapped Dez on the lips.

"Hush-a-tongue!"

Dez opened her mouth to scream, but not a sound came out. She put her hands to her throat.

Serena continued on as if nothing had happened. "If only you'd had less of your mama's upright temperament . . . who knows? A crying shame is what it is."

"Are you . . . going to kill me?" I choked on the words.

Serena clapped her hands and bellowed out a laugh. "Goodness, Nephew! Of course not! We learned long ago how important it is to have blood kin close by . . . in case you're ever needed."

I heard a noise behind me and spun around to see Agnes with a tin pail hanging from the crook of her parasol. She set it on top of the cage, on the bars directly over my head. Then she tipped the bucket over and stepped back quickly, her eyes lit up with menace.

A scraping noise came from inside the container—something was dragging itself toward the opening. I sunk back into a corner of the cage. Dez made a lunge toward the pail, meaning to knock it away. But Agnes was ready for her—she shoved Dez back with a jab of her parasol. Mabel came up behind Dez and snatched a fistful of her hair through the bars. I felt Dora's fingers wrap around my throat like a steel collar. She pulled me tight against the side of the cage.

A black shape, about the size of a man's head, lurched and bobbed out of the overturned pail. Spidery legs reached out, groping their way onto the cage bars above us.

"It's called a Tomb Creeper," said Agnes. "Very same one that got your folks."

"Don't worry," said Serena. "It won't hurt much. The poison works remarkably fast."

The Tomb Creeper latched tightly onto the cage with all its claws and began to pull at the bars. The metal creaked and groaned and, much to my horror, the bars began to bend. Dez and I kicked and struggled furiously, but the witching maids held us tight against the sides of the cage.

In a matter of seconds, the Tomb Creeper made an opening as wide as its shell. A bumpy black tail—like a scorpion's–uncoiled and touched its stinger to one of the bars. A silver thread appeared, like the silk spun by a spider, and the Tomb Creeper lowered itself through the hole into the cage.

Slowly, it twisted on its silver thread, bony legs clawing at the air, until the black shell came around to face us.

Dez let out a terrified shriek.

A human skull, hollow eyed and black as coal, hung in front of us.

The creature was using the skull as its shell!

"Hard to come by, Tomb Creepers," said Agnes, her eyes fixed gleefully on the beast. "Only grow in the skull of a witch that was murdered by her own kin."

"We've got your great-great grandma Arabella Farch to thank for growing this one," Serena added. "And her husband, Elthus, for providing the skull."

I clawed at Dora's stranglehold with all the fury I could summon.

The witching stick beneath my leg sent out a shock of heat–and my hand grabbed for it, as if by instinct. I raised it into the air, aimed it at the Tomb Creeper, and screamed at the top of my lungs–

"Blunderblast!"

The explosion was tremendous. A hundred times worse than the one I'd set off in the barn. There was no shower of boots this time. The sky filled with fire! Flaming rocks tumbled through the air. Streaks of *black* lightning, terrible and strange, shot down to the ground, blasting up earth across the barnyard. All around me was heat and wind and the sound of thundering stones. The whole world lit up in red.

Fiery rocks battered the bars above us, showering Dez and me with sparks and cinders–but the roof held up. My aunts and the witching maids were nowhere to be seen.

Then everything went quiet.

I sat there stunned and limp, gaping at what I'd done. The witching stick quivered in my hand. I dropped it to the floor of the cage, afraid of what else it might do. Fires burned all around. Smoke rose from the brimstone scattered across the ground.

But where was the Tomb Creeper?

I searched the cage, panicking, ashes raining down all around me. It was gone . . . vanished. . . .

Then I noticed Dez. Her eyes were wide with fright, fixed on a spot just over my shoulder. Her mouth moved wordlessly, still under the spell that Serena had used to silence her:

It's . . . by . . . your . . . neck!

A pair of enormous hands latched on to the cage from outside, and Dora pulled herself to her feet, smoke rising from her billowy dress. Mabel appeared next to her, eyes bulging with fury. Dead toads dangled from her hair. Agnes and Serena clambered from beneath the truck, their witching sticks raised. Their eyes were full of rage . . . and something else . . .

Fear.

A sharp pain shot through my neck–the sting of a thousand yellow jackets all at once. I shrieked, swatting at the creature with both hands. Dez joined in, too. But the Tomb Creeper held tight. Poison shot through my body like wildfire. Fighting back tears of pain, I grabbed hold of Dez's leg and pulled the boot from her foot. I struck the creature as hard as I could and sent it tumbling into the far corner of the cage. Its legs and tail coiled up in a flash, disappearing into the black skull.

But I was too late. The damage was done.

Dez wrapped her arms around me as I writhed in agony, knives coursing through my limbs. My toes and fingers were first to go numb. Then my ears . . . my nose . . . my lips. I turned my head to curse at Agnes and Serena, but my voice was lost.

I could only watch, horrified, as my skin and clothes turned gray. A rush of cold swept over me. I was being soaked through by the poison . . . turned into solid rock. I heard a muffled squeal behind me. I knew it was Dez, though I could no longer feel her.

"Look!" cried Agnes. "The girl is turning to stone, too!"

"That's impossible!" Serena's eyes went wide. "The Tomb Creeper didn't come near her."

"Must be from touching the boy," said Agnes.

Serena leaned forward. Behind me I heard the *tap-tap-tap* of her witching stick against rock. "Looks like the girl got a full dose of the magic just from holding on to him." She reached into the cage and picked up the witching stick I'd dropped. She turned it over in her hand, a mystified look on her face.

"And that spell he used on us . . ." Agnes eyed the stick as if it could bite. "Where in eternal blazes did he get that?"

Serena ran the back of her hand against my lifeless cheek. "Seems that our little nephew has a lot more of the gift than I ever thought possible. Such a shame, isn't it? Won't do him a bit of good now."

I stared back at her through granite eyes—motionless, soundless, helpless as a tombstone.

22

Bone Back & Belly Dragger

IT IS A DREADFUL THING TO BE MADE OF SOLID stone. To have every part of your body gone to sleep, dead to the world. Everything except your thoughts and senses. I could still see the world going on around me. I could hear it, I could long for it, but I was no longer part of it. Anyone looking at me would've thought I was nothing but a statue cut out of granite. They would've seen a scrawny farm kid, carved from stone, his mouth wide open in a petrified scream for all eternity. Worse than that, Dez was part of the statue, too. I couldn't feel her or see her, but I knew she was back there, holding on to me–the very last thing she did on this mortal earth before the Tomb Creeper poison turned her to rock.

The flatbed Ford bucked and sloshed over Moaning Marsh Road, plowing down Strangle Oaks as it went. From our cage, Dez and I had a clear view off the back. The moon shone bright as Agnes and Serena got into the Franklin. The witching maids tried to climb into the backseat, but Agnes swept them away with her parasol. Dora collapsed to the ground in tears—her sobs echoed across the marsh. Wherever Grobbs was headed, it appeared my aunts were coming along, too.

KA-BANG!

A cloud of black smoke shot from the Franklin's tailpipe. Agnes and Serena both sprang from the car. Curls of smoke rolled over the barnyard.

That's when Grobbs stomped on the gas pedal. Mud and water flew. Strangle Oaks hissed in fury as we mowed them over, leaves and branches bursting to pieces. We bounded across the marsh at a frightful clip. Dez and I were tossed back and forth against the walls of our cage as it strained at the ropes. The statues of Mama and Poppers clattered against the cauldron so violently I feared they'd crack.

My aunts grew smaller and smaller behind us. A feeling of hope welled up inside me. Grobbs was trying to make a getaway! He must've rigged up the Franklin to explode. Was he just trying to save himself and Jack? Or did he have a plan to turn us back to normal?

Maybe there was still a chance!

A fiery flash lit up the sky over my aunts' barnyard. A tremendous *BOOM!* shook the ground. A moment later, I heard a whooshing sound off in the distance. It grew louder and louder by the second. Even over the truck's thumping and splashing, I could hear it—like a howling windstorm.

Out of the darkness behind us, a black shape rose into

sight, hovering above the swamp. Something large. Unspeakably large. It was the Franklin. With steely wings beating against the air, it gained on us, heaving and roaring like a dragon. The headlights burned fiery red. A plume of blue smoke trailed behind it. Strangle Oaks burst into flames as it rumbled above them.

Grobbs forced another burst of speed from the truck, which sent it swerving across the road. Another couple minutes and we would've ended up at the bottom of the marsh. But the Franklin shot over us with a mighty roar, and our truck spun around, skidding to a stop.

Whether it was Grobbs that stopped us or some bewitchment by my aunts, I couldn't tell. But we'd turned clean around, and I found myself staring off the back of the truck into the Franklin's blazing headlights just as the ghastly contraption set down on the track. With its growling motor and belching smoke, the fire-breathing monstrosity looked half machine and half beast. It glared at us through the haze as if sizing up its next meal.

Grobbs stepped out into the muck and slogged around to the back of the truck, a hatchet in hand. Agnes and Serena leaped out of the Franklin with their witching sticks at the ready, glowing like hot pokers.

"I don't know if you can hear me, boy," Grobbs muttered as he passed by. "I done what I could. I'm sorry it turned out like this. You're on your own now."

He spat out a mouthful of licorice root and stepped toward the Franklin.

"Goodness' sakes, Mr. Grobbs," sniggered Serena. She was a black shadow, standing in the red glow of the headlights. "If I didn't know you were a man of your word, I'd almost think you were trying to cut out on your end of the bargain."

"I don't honor bargains with the devil," said Grobbs.

"What I want to know," said Agnes, "is what you expected to do with the boy and those other lumps of stone? Planning to conjure them back to flesh and blood, were you?"

"I don't give a pig's rump about your kin," said Grobbs. "I got no trust for Dredmoores, livin' or dead. Figured I'd better cut out before me and Jack ended up like them." He nodded toward me and the other statues. He shifted the hatchet in his hand like he was anxious to use it. "Me 'n Jack . . . that's all I care about. Good riddance to the rest of you."

Serena turned to Agnes. "Well, Sister, it seems Mr. Grobbs can no longer be trusted. Suppose I'll have to drive the truck myself, and you'll follow along in the Franklin."

Agnes jabbed her parasol into the mud. "You know I'm no good at driving automobiles. They always go into the ditch."

"You'll have to make the best of it. We can't be seen flying over the rooftops." Serena rapped her witching stick against the palm of her hand. "The next question is . . . what to do with our hired man?"

Agnes's witching stick let out a swell of purple light. "Let me tend to that," she said eagerly.

She stepped toward Grobbs, her eyes red as embers. Grobbs raised his hatchet and stood firm.

"You've been a nettle in my skin too long, Virgil Grobbs. I'm going to enjoy this more than–"

"Ar-ar-arooo!" There was a fierce growl, a flash of teeth, and Agnes stumbled backward, shrieking. The hound lunged for her legs . . . her arms. . . . She swung her witching stick at the dog and shouted:

"Slithering belly dragger!"

A flash of purple lit the sky. The dog dropped to the ground with a whelp. He writhed in the muck, howling and snapping. Brown smoke rose from his fur. Grobbs dropped his hatchet and sprang to the animal's side.

The smoke grew thick as tar, and even in my petrified state, I could smell the stench.

Then the dog began to shrink. He grew smaller and smaller by the second. His legs shriveled to nothing. His fur turned to slimy scales. Only the ears and tail remained–the rest of him looked like an overfed grass snake.

Serena burst out in laughter. "I declare, Agnes! You've certainly gone rusty with your witching stick, haven't you?"

Agnes opened her mouth to snap back, but Grobbs threw himself on her and knocked her to the ground. He knelt over her, clutched onto her throat with his one good hand, and started to squeeze.

Serena raised her witching stick and opened her mouth to speak–then stopped.

She stood for a while and watched, shaking her head in

amusement. For a minute I thought she was going to let Grobbs throttle her sister right there in the mud. But right when Agnes's face was turning from red to blue, Serena cracked Grobbs on the head with her witching stick and said:

"Snappish bone back!"

In a flash, Virgil Grobbs was no more. In his place was the most enormous snapping turtle I'd ever seen. Agnes shoved the creature off her chest with a groan. She coughed and gasped as Serena helped her to her feet. The turtle lay sprawled on its back in the muck, stubby legs clawing at the air, jaws snapping furiously.

Agnes rubbed her throat, glaring hatefully at her sister. She tried to shout, but only a raspy hiss came out.

Serena looked away, smirking. "Come along, Sister. We're late. Mustn't leave the others waiting."

Agnes stuck the toe of her shoe under the snapper's shell and gave him a kick. He rolled down the slope and into the marsh with a plop. The dog-eared snake slithered after him.

23

The Choosing

WE DROVE ALL NIGHT LONG AND ON PAST daybreak. I didn't sleep at all, rattling along on the back of the truck. At least I don't think I fell asleep. It's hard to tell when you can't so much as blink your eyes. The first awful shock had worn off, and now I'd settled into a deep despair. It felt like I had no body at all. I was a cloud of scared thoughts and misery stuck inside a big lump of granite.

Agnes had told the truth about her driving–she was a menace on wheels. Even worse than her sister. Serena had to stop every few miles to conjure the Franklin out of a ditch. Agnes got worse and worse as the night wore on, smashing into stop signs, mailboxes, and even a wagon full of cow manure. Serena got so irritated that she bewitched the car to make it float in the air. Then she towed it behind the truck at the end of a rope–a *long* rope on account of the smell.

Shortly after sunup, we came to the crossroads at Cold Creek Junction and turned up the track–the road to

The Witches of Dredmoore Hollow

Dredmoore Hollow! My hopes jumped a notch; I'm not sure why. Home or not, it would hardly matter while me and my folks were human tombstones.

Serena drove right past the house and across the barnyard, then up the old wagon road. My heart sunk. Those tracks led to only one place–my least favorite spot in Dredmoore Hollow.

We pulled up to the iron fence and stopped next to the cemetery gate. A shiny white Packard was parked there, up against the blackberry briars. I'd have known that showy thing anywhere. It belonged to the creepy little man I'd met at my aunts' place–Cousin Japeth–the one who'd made up all the hogwash about Blithering Brain Rot. Last time I saw that car, it was stacked from floor to roof with witching supplies.

"Dearest Serena!" sang a voice from the graveyard.

Cousin Japeth appeared from among the gravestones and hurried toward us. His face lit up at the sight of Serena. He pinched the ends of his mustache to smooth out the curls. Two gangly fellows loped along behind him. They looked alike as two berries on a bush, and an eeriesome pair, too–these had to be the Dredmoore twins that Serena had mentioned before. Each wore a long black oil coat and walked with a lean-forward gait. Their hair hung in ratty curtains over their faces so that only their beaky noses poked out.

"My lovely, lovely Serena!" chirped Cousin Japeth. "We were worried half out of our wits! Was it a gruelsome journey? You must be exhaustified!"

Serena let him kiss her hand. Her fox wrap gave a

shudder. The twins sauntered up and nodded. No one paid any mind to Agnes. She eyed each of them sourly.

"Cousin Seth, Cousin Silas," said Serena, donning her phoniest smile. "Sister and I truly do appreciate everything you've done. It's a wonder how you managed to hunt down all those potions and such overseas. I declare, you must've made friends with every dark warlock in England. We never could've broken the curse without your gallant deeds!"

The twins bowed their hairy heads and grunted something I couldn't make out. Japeth shot them a jealous look, tugging nervously at his mustache. The twins jostled past him to get a glimpse of the back of the truck.

The whole bunch of them gathered around the truck bed and stared at the cauldron in reverent silence. After a while, Japeth clasped his hands together and sighed. "Truly amazifying, Cousin Serena! Not a scratch on it! Or as the Italian folk say, *perfecto splendeeto!*"

The twins muttered in agreement.

None of them seemed to notice me or the other statues strapped to the back of the truck. Their eyes were fixed on the cauldron like it was a pot of gold.

"Well, let's not stand here ogling," said Agnes. "The sooner we get on with the Choosing Ceremony, the better."

Japeth coughed into his handkerchief in an attempt to disguise a chuckle. "I suppose you fancy you'll be the chosen one, Cousin Agnes?"

She turned on him in a flash and stuck the tip of her parasol up to his nose.

"As likely a chance as you, Cousin!"

The twins snorted in unison.

"Now, now," Serena cut in. "There's no call for bickering between family. We all ought to be celebrating!"

The others fell quiet, still glaring at each other. Serena continued on in a scolding tone. "Look what we've accomplished, the five of us! For fifteen years, we suffered the woes and humiliations of the Blighted Broomstick Curse. *Fifteen years!* A hex so powerful that the spellbooks said it couldn't be broken. Did we let that stop us? Did we throw up our hands in defeat? Of course not! We worked together! It's true that Sister and I were the ones that found the book with the Mending Brew. But what good would that've done if Japeth hadn't come up with the recipe for Bristle Sprout Tonic? Or if the twins hadn't brought back all those charms and potions from overseas? Why, there'd have been no witching maids . . . no Mending Brew . . . no restoring of the gift! We worked together like family should . . . and now the cauldron is *ours*! Think of it! This will be the first dark magic Choosing in a century! No matter who is chosen to be the Keeper of the cauldron, this is a glorious day for every one of us. We must join together and act like true-hearted kin."

There was an awkward silence while Serena's speech sunk in. Then the entire loathsome bunch hung their heads shamefully, until finally, Japeth dropped to his knees and gushed, "Oh, dearest Serena! We all know you'll be chosen anyway. That's how it *should* be!"

The twins nodded, and everyone embraced and patted each other on the back, acting all cozy again. Everyone except for Agnes. She skulked off into the graveyard muttering under her breath, whacking the heads off daisies with the tip of her parasol.

Serena floated the cauldron, dark and weightless as a storm cloud, into the graveyard. She ordered Japeth and the twins to haul me and the other statues in among the tombstones. The cousins didn't have too much control over their witching sticks just yet, so they had to carry us.

"Why don't you set them all near the statue of Phineas Dredmoore?" Serena instructed. "Not too close together . . . but enough so they can gaze fondly at each other, to help them bide the time. It's the least we can do—they *are* kin, after all."

The twins hoisted Dez and me onto their shoulders and stepped through the iron gate.

"Oh, cousins! I nearly forgot!" Serena called after them.

Seth and Silas stopped, staggering under the weight of us.

She lowered her voice to a whisper. "I'd walk very softly if I were you. I'm sure you recollect the Burrowing Ravenweed under the grass? The one that got Hester and Haimish a couple years back?"

The twins stood dead still, surveying the graveyard.

"Oh, there's nothing to worry about so long as you're careful," coaxed Serena. "Just tread gently and don't kick up any sod."

They turned and stared at her.

"Go on!" She shooed them along with a wave of her hand.

With Dez and me teetering on their shoulders, they tip-toed across the grass as if it was made of eggshells.

They brought all of us statues up to the middle of the cemetery and set us among the gravestones. In between us was the towering statue of Phineas Dredmoore on horse-back. The marker at the footstone said:

In honor of
Phineas Dredmoore
1724-1824
Who bravely led us hither
Through raging seas
and
Woeful blights of spirit

Forever shall we remember his wisdom:
Some Things You Choose.
Some Things Choose You.

I recognized that last part from the sampler hanging over the Victrola at home. I knew it had come from Phineas Dredmoore's gravestone, but I'd never given the words much thought. Now I had all eternity to ponder it over.

It certainly was a woeful state of affairs, being stuck there among the headstones of my long-dead kin. I was alive and not alive at the same time. I could see Mama and Poppers, and I supposed they could see me, too, and there was some comfort in that. But not much.

I knew my body was leaned back against Dez, with my stone head on her shoulder. But try as I might, I could neither see nor feel her. I'd only known her a few short days, and now we were stuck together till the end of earthly time.

Things might have come out differently if I'd only been quicker to use the witching stick . . . if I'd only shown a little more courage. This thought would haunt me forever. If Dez had been the one with the stick, she would've blasted the aunts and everyone in sight, first chance she got. True, she probably would've blown us both to pieces in the bargain . . . but at least she would've tried. If I'd only done *something . . . anything . . .* while I still had the chance, Mama and Poppers might be free. Dez and me, too. But I'd been too scared to try. Too doubtful of myself. And now, there was nobody left to be the hero.

The dark magic Dredmoores had won.

Agnes, Serena, and the others spent the day getting ready for the Choosing. The twins brought all the witching sundries up from the Franklin, while Serena ordered her sister and Japeth to prepare ingredients for the cauldron. It was clear that Serena had decided she was the one in charge. From my perch among the tombstones, I watched as she bossed the others around, lording over the cauldron and making all the decisions. She flashed that phony smile of hers and pretended to be everyone's best friend—but I could see that they were getting sick of her.

Japeth was up to tricks of his own. He snuck the twins off behind a gravestone near me, and I overheard him working a bargain.

"It seems to me," he whispered, "there's amplous likelihood the cauldron will choose one of *you* to be the Keeper! The spirits of the dark Dredmoores will recollect that Confoundence Curse you put on Ester way back when. Such brilliance! Such *viva la bonbon*, to quote the French! Not many could've done it, you know!"

Seth and Silas both stuck their chests out and exchanged congratulating glances.

"Now if either of you is chosen to be the Keeper," Japeth went on, "as I fully expecticate that you will be, I want you to know that my loyalty to you would be undying to my very last mortal breath. I would be as faithful a partner as you shall ever find. And you can both be sure that if I am chosen, I shall do likewise—it is my solemn vow! *Maximus oathus requiem!*"

He put a hand on each of the cousin's shoulders.

"Do we have an understanding, then?"

They nodded and they all shook hands, exchanging sinister grins. Then they slipped off in separate directions across the graveyard.

Not ten minutes later, I saw Japeth fawning after Serena, acting out the same speech, practically word for word. Judging by all the nodding and winking, she appeared to be just as agreeable to the scheme as the other two. Only Agnes was passed over in the secret wheedling. As the day grew on, she became more bad-tempered than ever—more withdrawn, irritable, suspicious . . . until she was the very picture of bitterness and spite.

When the sun finally set, Serena conjured a fire underneath the cauldron and began cooking some foul and fiendish brew. The air filled with smoke that made the oak leaves turn black and crumble to bits. Birds fell dead from the branches. The moon itself seemed to go blood red.

My aunts and cousins joined hands and began marching around the cauldron. As they moved, the flames grew higher, turning from red to purple to a deep, eerie blue. The group started chanting, their voices low and grim. The words of their incantation sent a tremor through my poor stony soul:

Fallow sow and rotted root,
Shriveled spleen and blighted fruit.
Dredmoore spirits, kith and kin,
Let the Choosing now begin.

Darkness is the path we set,
Darkness shall our pow'rs beget.
Choose a Keeper, keen and cruel,
Choose a Keeper, thee to rule.

The Witches of Dredmoore Hollow

Dredmoore spirits kith and kin,
Let the Choosing now begin.

Slowly, they circled the bubbling cauldron, mumbling their menacing refrain. Each time they went around, the blue flames leaped higher, the smoke turned darker, and the roar of the cauldron grew louder.

All of a sudden, a host of foggy forms appeared from the blackness. I couldn't figure where they'd all come from—they'd simply faded in. They were more shadow than body. One by one, they joined the circle, drifting over the grass, chanting in mournful, distant voices:

Dredmoore spirits kith and kin,
Let the Choosing now begin.

The impossible horror of it struck me full on: these were the spirits of my ancestors! The very worst of them! Just as my aunts had planned, their foul, restless souls had been called up for the Choosing.

I'd spent many a night over the years lying awake in worry of ghosts. But never in my most fearful nightmares had I imagined anything as ghastly as these Dredmoore ghouls. There was a tall one with a stovepipe hat and a devilish white smile; his head was twisted, facing the wrong way, and a broken-off noose hung around his neck. Another ghoul, big around as a springhouse, was shot full of arrows, and a rusty hatchet stuck out from the middle of his forehead.

A few of them rode upon broomsticks, and one with hollow eyes straddled a ghostly horse. Some were missing limbs and other parts. One headless fiend carried a cow's skull under his arm as if he'd gotten the raw end of a swap.

My aunts and cousins showed no fear. They moved aside, calm as could be, never breaking their chant and letting the spirits join the circle. Their bodies blurred right through each other so I no longer could tell the spirit Dredmoores from the living ones. It was a muddle of blue fire and smoke and whirling forms.

All at once, the five flesh-and-blood Dredmoores raised their witching sticks into the air. The tips blazed with the same blue light as the fire, setting the tombstones and treetops aglow.

Then one stick began to shine a deeper blue than all the others, changing slowly to a dark and raging violet–an eerie color, full of threat and doom. The violet glow spread wider and wider above its conjurer, and a smoldering shape took form in the sky:

The mark on the Dredmoore cauldron!

The shape grew larger and brighter, while the glow of the other four witching sticks grew dimmer and dimmer, until at last they died out. Then the spirits turned to fog and disappeared.

Serena and the others stared at the violet cloud in shock.

Their eyes followed the swirling trail of energy to its source . . . to the only witching stick that remained aglow. The same sinister shade of violet as her eyes.

Agnes had been chosen.

She was the Keeper of the cauldron now. . . . She controlled its magic and power.

She lowered her witching stick. The violet blaze faded to a soft gleam, but her eyes glowed brighter than ever. She stepped up to the cauldron and caressed it with a single, loving stroke.

No one spoke a word.

The horror on their faces told me all I needed to know: Agnes controlled all our fates now–Dredmoores fair and foul.

24

Stone to Bone

IT WAS ANOTHER LONG SLEEPLESS NIGHT. A numb feeling settled over me, as if I was fading away. Not tired so much as going dim, like a lantern running out of oil. It seemed as though even my thoughts were turning to stone.

I could see Mama and Poppers across the graveyard, orange moonlight falling over them. They'd been turned to statues for a while now. I hoped they could still see me. Maybe they were thinking about me, too. I couldn't help worrying that they'd been statues for too long . . . that they'd gone to stone on the inside. I knew that's what was happening to us. All of us. Little by little, we were fading. After a while, we'd stop feeling and thinking altogether, and we'd be nothing but rock through and through.

The sun had hardly peeked over Clabberclaw Mountain when Serena and Agnes came sauntering up the hill into the graveyard. Things had changed since the Choosing, that was clear enough. Agnes walked in the lead and Serena marched a few steps behind, head hung low, her face pale and wretched.

Agnes had a proud set to her jaw. Her cyclone hairdo was stiff as a mountain peak, her eyes dark and dangerous. She held her witching stick in one hand and a large, gray wishbone in the other, her parasol hooked over her arm. She stepped up and glared at me.

"I still don't see the point in it!" She turned to Serena. "I'm Keeper of the cauldron now. I've got no reason to be afraid of anyone."

"We don't want to take any chances, do we?" said Serena in a gentle tone. "I thought we'd agreed to a plan?"

"*Your* plan!" snapped Agnes. "That was before the Choosing. I'm the one in charge now."

"That's right, Sister," said Serena. "It's just that we decided–"

"*We* don't decide anything . . . not anymore!" Agnes's eyes went to slits. "It doesn't matter what the rest of you think. I have final say as far as the cauldron's concerned."

"Of course, Agnes dear." Serena grimaced. "It's entirely up to you."

It was unsettling to see Serena cowering to Agnes. I wondered just what awful powers Agnes had gained now that she'd been chosen.

"Well . . ." Agnes studied the wishbone with an impatient scowl. "The plan is already in the works. We may as well see it through."

"Whatever you think is best, Sister," said Serena.

Agnes held the bone over my head and tapped it with her witching stick—

"Stone to bone!"

A sprinkling of gray dust fell over me, and a violet flash lit up the graveyard. My whole body went to mush. I let out a cry as Dez and I flopped over in a jumble of arms and legs. We thrashed on the ground, twisted together, clumsy and useless. I tried to roll off her, but couldn't muster control over my limbs. My hands and feet felt like rubber. The sensation was horrible and wondrous at the same time. I could *feel* again! I was flesh and bone!

"You do the talking," commanded Agnes, shoving her sister in front of me. The wishbone disappeared into her parasol.

Serena propped us up against a tombstone. Then she stepped back and looked us over like we were a window display in the dry goods store.

"Agnes and I are dreadfully sorry we had to put you through that business with the Tomb Creeper." She shook her head remorsefully. Her fox wrap made a sniffling sound. "I know it must've been a terrible ordeal for you."

Dez tried to shout something, but her tongue wasn't working just yet, so the words came out—

"Uh ooo aeee!"

Serena smiled as if she understood, then continued on.

"We certainly never meant for your little friend here to get caught up in this, Elijah. But we couldn't abide having either of you on the loose till everything was said and done. Which it is now."

She nodded toward Agnes.

"Your aunt Agnes is Keeper of the Dredmoore cauldron now. The family gift is back, more powerful than ever. We've done everything necessary, and it can't be undone. Not ever again. So long as Agnes is master of the cauldron, her word is law."

Agnes stared down at me, clutching her parasol like a weapon. There was murder in her eyes. It didn't make sense that she'd set me free. She reached into her parasol, pulled out a funny-shaped bottle, and handed it to her sister.

"Hurry it up," she said. "We've got other matters to tend to."

The bottle was the same shape as Agnes's hairdo, tall and twisty. Through the glass I could see brown smoke full of tiny black flecks spinning 'round and 'round.

Serena set the bottle on the ground at my feet. Dez lunged forward with a holler, grabbing for Serena's witching stick. But she was still too weak and rubbery, and she flopped facedown in the grass. Serena sat Dez back against the tombstone and gave her a little pat on the head.

"Now that everything's settled," said Serena, "Agnes and I would like to set things right. It's true your mother put us through fifteen years of shameful agony. But it's time to put that behind us. We aren't the kind to hold a grudge."

Agnes's scowl said much to the contrary.

"Katrina is our sister, after all," chirped Serena. "And it's time we let bygones be bygones. Isn't that so, Agnes?"

Agnes gave a wincing nod.

"We sent word to Grandma Ester, telling her that your

mama would be needing her help. When she gets here, you just give her that bottle of Tomb Creeper Remedy, and she'll fix your folks up good as new. Easy as rhubarb pie, hmm?"

I shook my head frantically and tried to plead with her, but all that came out of my mouth were a few garbled grunts.

"We'd give them the remedy ourselves, of course, but I don't expect your mama's going to be too happy with us. It'll be best if we're not here when she turns back to flesh and blood, don't you agree?"

Serena paid no attention to my flailing arms and howls of protest.

"The poison will wear off directly," she said cheerfully. "You just rest up awhile and you'll see. One day all this will be behind us, and we'll look back and have a good laugh. Why, I'd wager that you and I will become good friends one day, Elijah."

She gazed at me wistfully and sighed.

Agnes let her hateful glare hang on me a while longer, then she turned and headed toward the cemetery gate. Serena bent down and kissed me on the forehead. She took hold of my hand.

"Don't you worry, Elijah," she said. "Your grandma Ester will be here in no time. Just make sure she gets that bottle of Tomb Creeper Remedy, and she'll have everyone as good as new before you know it!"

She stood and hurried down the hill, turning every few

steps to wave back at us. Dez and I flopped and writhed on the grass, calling after her in grunts and yelps.

The day rolled past and nighttime fell again, and still no sign of Grandma Ester. The feeling had gradually come back to my arms and legs, like Serena had said. As soon as we could stand up without toppling over, Dez and I wobbled our way out of the graveyard. We moved slow as cold molasses—just in case that Burrowing Ravenweed was still under the grass.

After that, there was nothing to do but wait for Grandma Ester. I'd hidden the bottle of remedy in the softest, safest place I could find—a mossy stump next to Mama's statue. I was scared to death it would get busted if I kept it in my pocket; then Mama and Poppers would be stuck in granite forever.

Dez and I gathered up sticks and built a good-sized fire outside the cemetery gate. Our plan was to sit awake all night till Grandma Ester came. I was sure she'd set off the minute she heard that Mama needed her help. It did occur to me, of course, that my aunts might not be telling the truth. Could be they'd never sent a telegram to Grandma Ester, and the bottle of remedy was a fake—why hadn't they left us one of those funny wishbones they used on Dez and me? Could be the whole thing was a lie. It sure wouldn't be the first time with those two. I just couldn't figure any other reason why they'd turned Dez and me back from stone.

Either way, Grandma would know what to do. She knew about witching . . . and about Agnes and Serena. Once she got ahold of that remedy, everything would be fine again.

At least I hoped it would.

The firelight danced on the tombstones. Only the night before, I'd seen the ghosts of the dark magic Dred-moores come seeping up from their graves. I tried to fight off the goose bumps by telling myself they'd only appeared on account of the Choosing. But my eyes searched the shadows restlessly, and I jumped at the slightest crack and rustle. I would've raced down to the lamp-lit warmth of the house in a heartbeat if it wasn't for Mama and Poppers. I just couldn't bear to leave them out there in the graveyard alone.

Naturally, Dez keeled over asleep the minute she sat down by the fire, and I was stuck there to bide my time alone. I almost would've preferred to be a statue again. There's nothing to make you feel so small and vulnerable as sitting out by a graveyard in the woods at night. I made as much noise as I could, stomping around and breaking sticks for the fire, but Dez went on snoring like she didn't have a worry in the world.

Worst of all was when the fire began to die down. In order to stoke it, I'd have to fetch more wood–and that meant feeling my way around in the forest . . . alone.

I scoured the ground and scraped together a few sorry twigs and some dead briar vines. Not enough to account for any kind of fire. Then something caught my eye a ways up the hill in the graveyard. The firelight was barely enough so that I could make out a big oak limb that had fallen near the cauldron.

I was none too anxious to go back into that graveyard, but the prospect of sitting in sheer darkness seemed a whole lot worse. So I stirred the fire, took a deep breath, and set off through the cemetery gate.

The limb was a beauty. Big and dry and sprawling with dead twigs and branches. I could see right off there'd be enough firewood to last the rest of the night. I hoisted the limb onto my shoulder—it weighed nearly as much as me—and made tracks back toward the fire as fast as my boots would carry me. Right as I came to the gate, I lost my grip. The back end of my load dropped to the ground, slashing a rut in the grass.

A black streak shot up through the sod . . . a shrill cry filled the air . . . a furious flutter of wings sounded all around me. I reeled, stumbling under the weight of the limb. The sky became a tempest of dirt and stones. . . .

Burrowing Ravenweed!

In my hurry to build up the fire, I'd forgotten about the monstrous vines. Black talons slashed out at me. I screamed as the oak limb on my shoulder burst to pieces. If it wasn't for the tangle of oak branches over my head, I would've been struck down on the spot.

Screaming and stumbling, twigs and wood chips showering all around me, I hurled myself out through the cemetery gate and beyond the Ravenweed's reach.

25

Whirlawings

I SAT THE REST OF THE NIGHT, A FAT STICK IN each hand, peering through the cemetery gate for any sign of Ravenweed. Had Mama known that thing was living in the family graveyard all this time? Anything seemed possible now that I knew about her secret. *Our* secret. What other horrors and mysteries had she kept from me? A swell of anger tightened my throat and rushed the blood to my face. But when I let my eyes drift up the hill to Mama's statue, the rage faded away. No matter what she'd kept from me, all I wanted was to bring her and Poppers back, to see them flesh and blood again.

There was no telling whether that would ever happen.

The only thing I could find nearby to burn was a patch of dried-up blackberry briars. They left my hands scratched up and bleeding, but that was a small price to pay for keeping the fire ablaze. Dez snored through the whole affair with hardly a stir.

I must have nodded off around sunrise. I'd hardly closed my eyes when I was jolted out of my sleep. Dez knelt next to me with her hand over my mouth. Her eyes searched the graveyard frantically.

"Listen!" she whispered. "There's something out there!"

A gushing sound came from somewhere beyond the cemetery, growing louder by the second.

Whooooosh!

I searched the shadows of the forest. Dez grabbed my arm.

Whoosh-hoosh!

It was closing in fast . . . whatever it was. A dark shadow slipped through the treetops.

Suddenly, a great round shape blotted out the sun and the whole graveyard went dark. Dez and I stumbled to our feet, gasping, ready to run.

Then the thing lifted up over the treetops, and I realized what it was. . . .

Grandma Ester's hot-air balloon!

I was never so happy to see a person in all my life.

Grandma Ester leaned over the edge of the basket and waved. She was wearing her leather flying jacket and goggles. Her hair was so wind-whipped it looked like she'd been electrocuted.

"Ho there, Elijah!" she called. "Stay put! I'm coming down directly!"

The balloon let out a long, howling *whoooosh* and dropped from the sky like a rock. The basket crashed onto the grass a short ways from the graveyard, and Grandma Ester clambered out with a cheery salute. She peeled off her jacket and goggles and straightened her skirts. Then she pulled a black shawl up over her shoulders.

Dez and I ran toward her, frantic and hollering.

"I came as soon as I got your mama's letter," she said, throwing her arms around me. "What the dickens are you doing up here by the graveyard? Last I knew, you wouldn't come within spitting distance of this place."

She pinched a pair of spectacles onto her nose and studied Dez for a moment.

"And who's this? You must be Eli's sweetheart, I gather?"

Dez's ears went bright red, and no doubt mine did the same.

"No . . . this is Dez," I said. Dez and I avoided each other's eyes. "We just met a few days ago up at Aunt Serena's place–"

"Serena?" Grandma Ester's voice went serious. "You've seen your aunt Serena?"

"Yes, ma'am," said Dez. "Up on Moaning Marsh. She and Agnes are both *witches*! *Black magic* witches!"

Grandma Ester's face turned deathly pale. She peered at me over the top of her spectacles. "Then . . . then you know about . . . ?"

I nodded, angry heat rising to my face again. "I know about the family gift . . . the cauldron . . . the curse . . . all of it."

"I'm sorry, Elijah," she said, her voice a strained whisper. She shook her head. "Your mama and I always wanted to tell you, but . . . well . . . we hoped we wouldn't have to. We thought the curse put an end to it all . . . to Serena and the others and their dark schemes. You were always such a worrier . . . such a nervous child. We thought you'd be better off if you never knew."

Better off if I never knew about my own family?

About a gift that ran through my own blood?

I wanted to scream and tell her how wrong she was—both her and Mama—but there was no time for it now.

I reached for her hand. "You've got to help us. . . . Serena and Agnes mended the cauldron. They held a Choosing Ceremony right here in the graveyard!"

"A . . . what? A *Choosing?*" She looked as if she might fall over.

"Dez and I saw the whole thing."

"Agnes got chosen," said Dez. "She's in charge of the cauldron now!"

Grandma Ester glanced back and forth between Dez and me. "But . . . but . . . your mama's letter . . . I got it just yesterday."

She pulled an envelope from her pocket and unfolded the paper:

Dear Mama,

I've got some wonderful news! You probably noticed that your witching powers came back out of the blue. I will tell you why—I found a way to mend the Dredmoore cauldron so it will never again conjure dark magic! There is no need to worry about Serena and Agnes and the other family scoundrels ever again. I have already used the cauldron to do all sorts of helpful deeds around Cold Creek Junction, and it is working better than ever. I mixed a potion to cure the boil off Matilda Teech's nose, and I got rid of the Plinketts' potato blight. It is a grand and marvelous thing to be using the family gift once again to help folks in need. Come down to the farm and we can celebrate! Tomorrow bright and early, if you can!

Your dearest daughter,

Katrina

"This letter's a trick," I said, handing the note back to Grandma Ester.

Dez lifted her golf cap and pulled the magic quill from her frizzy hair.

"Serena can conjure a magic quill to write like anyone she wants," I explained. "She used the same trick on me. Then I found out she'd turned Mama and Poppers to stone."

"Bit by a Tomb Creeper," added Dez. "They did it to me and Elijah, too. But the sisters turned us back again–"

"Mama and Poppers are in there. . . ." I pointed to the graveyard. "They've been frozen in granite for days. I'm worried we might be too late. . . . They . . . They might never be right again."

Grandma Ester gazed toward the cemetery, her jaw set hard, fire in her eyes.

"Where are Serena and Agnes right now?" she asked.

"Gone," said Dez. "They drove off with Japeth and the twins."

"Seth and Silas?" Grandma spoke the names as if they put a bad taste in her mouth.

"We've got to hurry," I pleaded.

I led the way up the hill. Grandma Ester peered around nervously, as if we were being watched. I stopped at the cemetery gate and took her arm.

"Wait!" I whispered. "There's something living under the ground . . . Burrowing Ravenweed, it's called."

Grandma Ester nodded. "I helped your mother put it there. It won't bother us so long as we walk softly."

She stepped through the gate and started slowly across the grass. Dez padded right along next to her. I swallowed hard and tiptoed after them, taking each footstep like I was walking on broken glass.

Grandma Ester's eyes scoured the graveyard. The fear on her face startled me—I'd never seen her show the least bit of worry about anything. It was clear she suspected there might be something even more dangerous than Ravenweed out here. I moved close to her side and so did Dez.

She stopped abruptly when we came in sight of the cauldron. A few wisps of smoke hung in the air in front of Phineas Dredmoore. Grandma Ester put her hand on my shoulder, signaling me to hold still.

"Mama and Poppers are over there." I pointed toward the other side of the cauldron.

Grandma stood motionless, but her gaze moved among

the tombstones as if she expected them to burst to life any second.

After a long while, we crossed the grass to Mama's statue. Tears welled in Grandma's eyes as she reached out to touch my mother's granite cheek. I knelt down to fetch the Tomb Creeper Remedy from its hiding place in the hollow stump. I was glad Grandma would be opening that tonic instead of me. Inside the bottle, the brown smoke still spun in circles like a miniature twister.

"Grandma," I whispered, tapping her on the shoulder as I held up the bottle. "Serena left this for you."

Grandma turned toward me and startled. Her spectacles flew from her nose.

"No, Elijah! That bottle's full of Whirlawings!"

She sprang back, stumbling, and pulled a witching stick from beneath her shawl. At the same moment, the stopper shot from the bottle, and a howling gush of brown smoke shot into the sky. The blast threw me backward, and the bottle flew from my hand.

What had I done?

The smoke spun furiously toward Grandma Ester, knocking her against a tombstone. Her witching stick hurtled across the graveyard.

There were dark shapes in the smoke . . . darting and fluttering. Bats! A whole swarm of them! Ghostly wings and fiery eyes, as weightless as dust themselves.

The whirlwind snatched Grandma Ester into the air and spun her around like she was made of feathers. The noise was deafening—the rushing wind, the howl and rumble.

Dez snatched up a tree branch and sprang toward the twister with a shout. I made a grab for her, but too late. A shadowy whip broke loose from the swarm—a streak of ghostly wings and ember eyes. The blow knocked Dez clear off the ground. I leaped to catch her and went crashing to the ground beneath her.

I rolled her onto the grass and lifted her head onto my lap. She had a bloody gash across her cheek, her face as white as milk. Twigs and dirt rained down on us as the cyclone churned up everything in its path.

Through a curtain of dust and grit, I could see Grandma Ester, trapped in the middle of the whirlwind. The swarm of bats closed in tighter and tighter around her. She clutched at her throat, gasping for breath.

They were killing her.

What could I do?

Mama and Poppers in stone . . . Grandma Ester being suffocated . . . Dez knocked unconscious or worse. I fought back the rush of panic swelling in my chest. My eyes fell on something in the grass just a short ways away. . . .

Grandma Ester's witching stick!

I had to try.

I braced myself against the wind, ready to make a run for the stick.

Then a voice came from behind me.

"I'm grievously sorry it had to come to this, Nephew. I truly am."

I turned to see Serena frowning down at me. Agnes stood beside her, eyes fixed on Grandma Ester churning inside the cloud of bats. Japeth and the twins appeared from behind a cluster of tombstones, witching sticks in their hands, their collars turned up against the pelting dust.

Fire shot through my limbs. I stood and faced Serena, so full of hate and fury I couldn't speak.

"It was a cruel trick," she said. "I'm not proud of it. I truly wish there'd been another way."

"You meant for this to happen!" I screamed. "You knew those *creatures* would attack her!"

"Whirlawings, they're called," Agnes said absently, her eyes locked on Grandma. "The ghosts of a thousand bats buried alive."

"It had to be done," said Serena with a sigh, wind whipping her hair like tongues of fire. "Your grandma's a great deal more dangerous than she looks. Used to be Keeper of the cauldron. She could out-conjure the best of us back in her day. Kept the dark magic Dredmoores in their place, she did. Hard to believe, isn't it? Now that Agnes has been chosen, we ought to have the edge, of course. But why take chances? We knew your grandma would trust you. You did exactly what we—"

"You're killing her!" I screamed. "Your own mother!"

Serena lowered her head against the growing wind. She took a few steps back, brushed the grit from her dress, and pulled up her fox wrap to cover her ears and chin. Japeth and the twins stood transfixed by the howling swarm of bats and debris, their arms raised to protect their faces. Agnes looked as if she'd gone into a trance. One eye twitched frightfully. Her face darkened with hatred . . . fear . . . confusion. I couldn't tell which. She pulled a witching stick from her parasol, and for a minute I thought she was going to blast the Whirlawings to pieces.

"Look what's become of you, Mama," Agnes murmured, her voice shaking. "To think you were the Keeper before me. Now here you are, helpless as a fly. I could do whatever I want to you."

"Sister," said Serena nervously, "don't forget, now . . . we all agreed on a plan. Why don't you put that witching stick away?"

Agnes stepped closer to the whirlwind. "Katrina would've been Keeper next if you'd had your way . . . or even Serena, if she'd only turned out like you hoped. Not me, though. No matter what I did . . . it never would be me."

"Agnes . . . please, Sister."

"Must be quite a surprise, isn't it, Mother?" Agnes bared her teeth. "Me . . . master of the cauldron! Me, with final say over *everyone*! Not Serena. Not the others. *Me!* What do you think of that?"

Suddenly Agnes snapped her witching stick forward and a stream of black smoke shot from the tip, wrapping the Whirlawings with a smoldering lasso. The swarm gave a powerful lurch, fighting to bust free, but Agnes held tight. She pulled back on her stick and the swarm jerked toward her. A thousand shrill cries filled the air.

"Sister!" cried Serena. "What are you doing?"

Japeth tried to grab Agnes's arm, but she shook him off.

"Don't be a fool!" he pleaded. "You'll disrupticate the Whirlawings!"

"I want to see her face," muttered Agnes, her lips trembling. "I want to see her eyes when she breathes her last breath."

She clung to her witching stick with both hands, struggling to keep control.

"Stop!" Serena trembled with rage. She drew out her own witching stick.

"I'm the Keeper!" roared Agnes. "I'll do as I please!"

A crackling explosion shook the ground. A blast of light sent Agnes hurtling through the air. She slammed against a rotting tree stump, let out a muffled cry, and slumped to the ground.

I turned to see Japeth with his witching stick raised. Smoke winnowed from the tip. His face was purple and quivering.

The whirlwind burst apart, and the bats scattered into the treetops. Grandma Ester dropped to the ground, limp and pale. I sprang toward her as a chorus of beastly screeches sounded from above.

The Whirlawings dropped from all corners of the sky and rushed together in a howling crash, even more fierce and violent than before. They bore down on the first thing they saw.

Japeth let out a high-pitched shriek and shoved Serena

into the Whirlawings' path. The twister snatched her from the ground like a toy, her fox wrap yowling, struggling to break free.

Japeth tried to run, but he'd hardly gone two steps before the cyclone caught him. It ripped the white jacket from his back . . . then his shirt . . . then his pants, and finally, the swarm swept his feet from beneath him and sucked him up into the roiling frenzy.

Seth and Silas nearly made it to the cemetery gate–they screamed in duet as the Whirlawings gobbled them up.

I knelt down beside Grandma Ester. Her eyes were closed, but she was breathing. A few yards away, Dez moaned and rolled over in the grass. I could try to drag the two of them to someplace safer. But how far would I get before those devilish Whirlawings came after us, too?

Then my eye fell on Grandma Ester's witching stick, still lying in the grass where it had fallen. The tip was glowing the slightest bit, soft and golden. Almost like it was calling to me.

26

A Flock of Ravens

THE DREDMOORE SCOUNDRELS SPUN HIGH IN the air, helpless as insects in the hold of the raging Whirlawings. They clung to their throats, gasping and gagging, eyes wide with fright. I watched from behind a mossy tombstone, clutching tight to Grandma Ester's witching stick. There was no good choice that I could see. If I tried to help, they'd most likely turn on me again—if the swarm didn't get me first. But if I didn't do something soon, they'd all be killed. They were my kin, after all. No one deserved such a dreadful end. Not even Agnes.

The witching stick pulsed in my hand, heavy as a heartbeat. I clenched my teeth and braced myself for the fool thing I was fixing to do.

Then, out of nowhere, a shout rang out—I nearly dropped the witching stick in surprise—and a violet fireball blazed across the graveyard. It slammed into the Whirlawings with a tremendous *BOOM!* The cyclone exploded, shooting fire-eyed bats in all directions. The air filled with sputtering sounds, and one by one their shadowy forms faded from the sky.

The graveyard went quiet.

Serena and the others had tumbled into a thick tangle of briars. They sprawled in the bramble coughing and wheezing. I peeked over the tombstone to see who'd conjured the fireball—and there stood Agnes. Smoke rose from the end of her witching stick.

"Where did the boy go?" Agnes limped toward the others, wincing in pain.

Serena struggled to her feet, plucking bits of briar from her skirt and hair. The fox wrap sneezed a cloud of dust.

"Thank you kindly, Sister," mumbled Serena. "Seems you saved us all from a most unpleasant end."

"Seems so." Agnes sneered.

Cousin Japeth fought his way out of the thicket, cursing and moaning. Agnes met his eyes with a fierce glare.

He quickly turned his gaze to the ground. "Oh . . . C-C-Cousin Agnes! I . . . I . . . sincerely do apologize for the inexcusable conjuration—"

Agnes cut him off with a flash of her witching stick—a bolt of purple lightning struck Japeth between the eyes and threw him hard against a tombstone. He slid to the grass with a whimper.

Agnes glowered at the twins. They quickly looked away, heads hung low.

"The boy couldn't have gotten far," said Serena. "We'd

better get him turned back to stone before he causes any trouble. Once we've put him and Mama in their final resting places, we can get on with our business." She turned quickly to Agnes. "Providing that's what *you* think we should do, Sister?"

Agnes narrowed her eyes. "I'm not so fixed on having the boy in stone as you are. Seems to me we'd be better off with him out of the way altogether."

That was all I needed to hear.

I tucked the witching stick into my pocket and lit off through the graveyard. I stayed low and snuck along behind the tombstones. I aimed for the Plinkett farm down in the valley. If Mr. Plinkett or the boys were home, we could drive to Cold Creek Junction for help . . . the police . . . the constable . . . somebody. Dez and Grandma Ester were counting on me. As for Mama and Poppers . . . I tried not to think about them . . . not right now.

A shout sounded across the graveyard. "There he is! Headed down the hill!"

I dropped to the ground, my heart pounding like a freight train. I drew out the witching stick and felt its warmth in my fingers. *What was I thinking?* I'd seen Agnes knock Japeth across the graveyard with a purple fireball. What chance did I have against her? Never mind that there were *five* of them. I didn't know the first thing about using a witching stick. The best I'd ever done was conjure a bunch of hot stones from the sky . . . *by mistake.*

The stick twitched to the left, pulling my hand along with it.

Was it trying to tell me something?

Breathless with fright, I crawled on my belly in the direction the stick pointed: straight toward the cauldron.

Was it leading me into a trap?

No . . . it couldn't be . . . could it? This was Grandma Ester's witching stick.

Then again . . . Agnes was Keeper of the cauldron now. Didn't she say she had control over all the conjuring? For all I knew, she even had control over Grandma's witching stick!

The stick lurched in my hand, tugging me toward the cauldron.

Did I dare trust it?

I pushed down my fear. I needed to think.

There was no way Agnes would be clever enough to bewitch Grandma Ester's stick—not without Serena suggesting it first. Odds were, it had never even crossed their minds.

I had to trust the witching stick. *I had to.*

Stones cut at my knees and thistles bit into my hands. I crept closer and closer to the cauldron. The statue of Phineas Dredmoore rose over me, fearless and strong— the sight of him raised my courage. I knew the cauldron was just on the other side of his horse. The witching stick pointed straight at him and pulsed.

What did it want me to do?

Was it pointing at the cauldron? Or at the statue of Phineas Dredmoore?

Voices whispered nearby. Boots on the grass. They were closing in around me. They'd find me any second.

Beneath me, the ground gave a tremble. Something rumbled through the earth, lifting the sod in a long, narrow lump. It rolled past me like an ocean wave, then settled and went still.

Burrowing Ravenweed!

The murderous stuff was everywhere in that graveyard. One wrong move, and I'd be smothered in vines and talons.

"I see him!" hollered one of the cousins. "In back of the statue!"

"Go get him then!" shouted Agnes.

"Try not to kill him," added Serena. "If you can help it."

Shouts rang out from all directions. The clamor of footsteps. I lay motionless, the witching stick like fire in my hand. Ravenweed slithered all around me beneath the sod, just waiting for someone to make a stumble.

I looked up at the statue of Phineas Dredmoore, towering high above the grass . . . beckoning.

I knew I was no match against my aunts' conjuring. But that didn't matter—I only needed to be *smarter* than they were. I only needed a better plan. I'd made a witching stick work twice before. I'd made it rain fiery stones. I had no idea whether I could do it again. But if I *could* . . . I was sure about what lay hidden under the graveyard. And one spell would be enough.

I closed my eyes and swallowed hard. The witching stick sent a warm tingle through my hand as if to coax me on.

I sprung to my feet and ran toward the statue. A single leap and I was on the back of Phineas Dredmoore's horse. I scrambled up onto my great-great-great grandpa's granite shoulders, climbing as far above the cemetery grass as I could.

Then I raised my witching stick and pointed it square down at Serena and Agnes.

"Look out!" shouted Japeth, his face red with blisters from Agnes's lightning bolt.

My aunts stared up at me in bewilderment.

I opened my mouth to shout, and a fit of dizziness rushed over me. The stick quivered in my hand. My mind went blank. I'd forgotten the conjure words.

"Goodness, Sister," said Serena. Her one sharp tooth bit into her smile. "Seems our nephew has found himself another witching stick."

Agnes lifted her own stick into the air, a sickening glee in her eyes. "I must say . . . I'm impressed, Nephew. Never figured you'd have the courage to fight back. Sad thing is . . . you should've stuck to being a coward."

She pointed her parasol at the black cauldron below me.

"That's *my* cauldron, right there. Did you know that? Chose *me* to be in charge of the entire Dredmoore family. My magic is most powerful. My word is final. The cauldron does what *I* say."

She paused to let the words sink in.

"Do you truly think a no-account little brat like you could possibly harm *me*?" She nodded toward the statues of Mama and Poppers. "You're as weak and foolish as your mama, and nothing will make me happier than to finish off the whole lot of you!"

The fiendish gleam in her eyes.

The poison in her voice.

The wicked joy on her face as she leered at Mama's statue.

Anger swelled through me like a dam bursting. I pointed my witching stick and my tongue came loose–

"BLUNDERBLAST!"

All at once the sky exploded. Crackling black thunderbolts tore through the air. Fiery brimstone stormed down. The ground burst apart like it was under cannon fire. Sod and dirt filled the sky. A plume of black smoke choked out the sun.

My aunts froze in shock for a split second–then they leaped for shelter among the tombstones. Flaming rocks pounded the graveyard, and I lost sight of them for a minute. I clung to Phineas Dredmoore's neck, gasping, shaking, barely able to hold on. The witching stick slipped from my fingers and clattered into the cauldron below me.

The firestorm stopped as suddenly as it had started. The graveyard was lost in a blanket of smoke. The only sounds were the crackle of a burning briar patch and the muffled groans of the twins and Japeth, buried somewhere in the rubble.

Agnes and Serena pulled themselves out of a collapsed grave, twigs and burnt leaves clinging to their hair. They struggled to their feet, witching sticks raised. A trickle of blood ran down Serena's cheek like a tear. She forced her lips into a quivering smile. She pointed her witching stick at me and opened her mouth to speak. . . .

But before she could say the conjure words, a streak of black vine shot into the air behind her. Black talons snapped down on her like a whip.

The air went wild with Ravenweed.

Clawed shoots burst from the ground all around the graveyard. Hundreds of them. The drumming of their wings shook the earth.

I clung to Phineas Dredmoore, motionless as a statue myself, in hope that the Ravenweed wouldn't notice me. My plan had worked better than I'd ever thought possible. Thrashing talons and slashing vines battered the grave-yard. The Ravenweed latched onto anything that moved–first Serena, then Agnes, then Silas, Seth, and Japeth. They screamed and clutched at the grass as the vines dragged them across the graveyard. Then, one by one, they disappeared beneath the sod. Their cries were unbearable. Oily black smoke poured from the Ravenweed holes. I held my shirt sleeve over my mouth and nose.

When the last of the shoots sunk into the ground, I climbed down from Phineas Dredmoore's statue and peered around the cemetery. I could see Grandma Ester trying to sit up in the grass at the far end of the graveyard. Dez lay a few feet away from her, rubbing her head. My heart jumped at the sight of them.

I was about to call out when a fluttering blur rose up in front of me. I threw my arms around the statue again, fearing the Ravenweed had come back for more.

"Haw haw!"

Five ravens climbed into the air, soot black, their wings pounding crazily. They were shamefully bad fliers, the whole bunch of them. They wobbled and spun, thumping into trees and gravestones, cackling and snapping at each other midair in a quarrelsome frenzy. Black feathers fell from the sky like October leaves. One of them—with a cyclone swirl of feathers on its head—circled toward me, squawking furiously. But the others shot after it, beaks and talons flashing, and finally, the whole lot of them fluttered off above Plinketts' orchard, scrapping and squabbling until they faded out of sight.

27

The Dredmoore Gift

G<small>RANDMA</small> E<small>STER</small> <small>HAD SOME TROUBLE COMING</small> up with a remedy to bring Mama and Poppers back to normal. She said her recollection of herbs and tonics had gotten rusty over the last fifteen years, and she was no use without her book of potion recipes. So I dug through every crate and sack in the Franklin until I found a pair of giant wishbones like the ones my aunts had used to cure Dez and me from the Tomb Creeper poison.

I was worried they might not work for Grandma Ester now that Agnes was Keeper of the cauldron. But Grandma said they ought to work just fine.

"The Choosing was most likely undone when Agnes got turned into a raven," Grandma said. She held up one of the wishbones. "Either way, she's in no state to meddle with us now."

Despite her confident talk, she was solemn and shaking as she cracked open the wishbones and sprinkled dust onto the two statues. Dez took my hand. We both held our breath.

A few seconds later, a wash of color spread over the statues, and Mama and Poppers both flopped to the ground, flesh and blood once again!

My eyes watered up with tears of joy. I'm not ashamed to admit it–I'd never been so happy.

As soon as the poison wore off a bit more, Mama wrapped her arms around me and hugged me clumsily. I had to hold her up.

"I'm so proud of you, Eli!" she said. "If it weren't for you, we'd all be . . ."

She couldn't say it. She just clutched me tight and kissed me over and over. Dez pretended not to watch, embarrassed for me, most likely. But I didn't care in the least.

"It was the cleverest thing I ever saw," Mama went on after a bit. "Conjuring those brimstones down on the grave-yard so the Ravenweed would attack! What was that spell word? I never heard it before."

I shrugged my shoulders and pretended that I couldn't recall. Truth was, I didn't know how to feel about the whole thing–being able to summon such power with a single word.

I had questions of my own that needed answering.

Mama's face glowed as she pulled me into her arms one more time. The questions could wait.

Poppers didn't come around quite so fast. He didn't know how to fight off the effects of the poison like Mama did, so it had settled into his brain pretty good. Grandma Ester said he'd probably act like a lump of stone for several weeks to come. Mama thought that might be just as well since she wasn't quite sure how to explain things to him at the moment.

"You really should've told Horace about the gift right from the start," said Grandma Ester. "After all these years, this is a fine way for him to find out the truth."

Mama shook her head. "You're right. . . . It was foolish of me to think I could keep it a secret forever."

Then she gazed affectionately down at Poppers, stiff as a log in the grass, and added: "On the other hand, Horace won't believe a word of this, anyway. He'll snort like a mule and tell me to quit talking nonsense. You wait and see what he says when he gets better. He'll claim it was nothing but a nasty bout of influenza."

She put Poppers to bed in the backseat of the Franklin with a wet rag over his head, hoping it would help bring him around. But he kept tumbling out of the car and curling up next to the cemetery fence, still as a fieldstone.

Two genuinely great things came out of my time on Moaning Marsh. For one, Mama made Poppers keep the Franklin. She told him we were tending to it till her sisters got back from "a long trip abroad." She had tried telling him the truth—with only a few minor alterations—but as she predicted, he rolled his eyes and wrote the whole story off as "poppycock and pig feathers."

He refused to drive the car, or even so much as touch it. "Automobiles will be the ruination of modern man!" he proclaimed, glaring at the thing as if he expected it to lunge at him. "They are against the natural order of things. Mark my words—we'll all live to rue the day!"

Well, Mama and I didn't do much ruing, I can tell you that much. It was a fine and splendid thing to motor about in a Series Eleven Franklin with a genuine air-cooled engine! Our very own car! And Mama was a crackerjack driver, too. Poppers didn't know what he was missing. He'd always told me the best way to get over your fears was to look them square in the eye; but every time we fired up the Franklin's motor, Poppers made a beeline for the barn.

The other good thing that came from my adventures was my new friend, Dez. Even though she lived way up in Blossom Springs, a whole day's drive by car, we promised to stay friends and write letters every week.

We'd hardly settled back at home when Mama told me that she and Grandma Ester were heading back to Moaning Marsh to "take care of some unresolved matters." I asked if I could come along, figuring I'd spend the whole time with Dez. Then I found out they'd be taking Grandma's hot-air balloon.

"Oh, you'll love it, Elijah!" Grandma assured me. "Once you're up in the air, you won't think about anything but how wonderful it is. The woods and villages down below! The wind in your face! There's nothing like it in all the world!"

The last thing I wanted was to act like Poppers did about the Franklin, so I choked back my panic and held my tongue. Then I found out what *Hodgeworth's Encyclopedia* had to say about the matter (volume B, page 57):

Hot-air ballooning is dangerous to the point of mortal folly, for the vehicle is subject to the mercies of the winds and cannot stay aloft without a perpetual flow of well-heated air to the entire balloon. The craft offers its pilot no navigational control whatsoever outside of vertical movement and requires the accommodation of a wide open space to achieve a hospitable landing.

When I showed this scholarly warning to Grandma Ester, she raised her eyebrows and gave me a crafty grin. As it turned out, her balloon didn't work at all like the regular kind—at least not now that the curse was lifted. The contraption was powered by something she called Aerial Locomotion Potion, brewed from curdled sparrow's milk, dragonfly tails, and other colorful ingredients of the sort.

You'd think I would've dreaded going back to Moaning Marsh after all that Agnes and Serena had put me through, but I could hardly wait. I was anxious to see Dez again, even though it had only been a couple days. But there was something else, too. A lot had changed since I'd first arrived at my aunts' place. The thought of Moaning Marsh still put a chill in my blood, but not like before. I felt like I was going back to settle some unfinished business of my own—maybe just to look the place in the eye and show it I'd won.

Grandma Ester was right about riding in a hot-air balloon. For the first few minutes I couldn't bring myself to look down over the edge . . . but once I did . . . *hot dandy!* Mama, Grandma, and I gazed down on the world in wonder, our arms slung over each other's shoulders, watching the hills and valleys roll away beneath us. No one spoke for a long while.

I still had a great many questions for both of them— nearly twelve years' worth of secrets and mysteries that needed explaining. I knew they'd only been trying to protect me, but the thought of it—all that time in the dark, not knowing the truth about myself—I couldn't help but feel hurt and angry.

Still, all of that could wait till later. I wasn't about to spoil the moment: the three of us aloft, soaring through the skies by magic, the Dredmoore gift coursing through our veins. Isn't family a strange and wondrous thing?

Dez got on with Mama and Grandma Ester like they were her own kin. She had no witching gift of her own, which was maybe for the best, considering her disposition. No matter, she joined right in, helping Mama and Grandma mix up potions and remedies and so forth. Agnes and Serena had made a colossal mess of things with all their dark witchery, and Mama said it was our obligation to set things right again.

It took three full hours to track down Virgil Grobbs and Jack. They were still changed into a snapping turtle and a dog-eared snake, skulking around in the swamp. Grobbs had eaten nothing but worms and bullfrogs since my aunts bewitched him. So he was deeply obliged to Grandma Ester and Mama. Poor Jack had been changed into so many different critters by now that he didn't know whether to hiss, howl, or heel.

The three witching maids had been left to their own doings all this time, so the place was a shambles. They'd flown through my aunts' house on their wobbling broomsticks. Every last window was shattered and hardly a door stood on its hinges.

After considerable digging through my aunts' witching supplies, Mama found the proper remedy and turned the witching maids back to their old selves. But no amount of conjuring could get the toads to stop following Mabel. Nor did she seem to mind.

"Magic can only go so far against the natural order of things," exclaimed Grandma Ester.

The last rescue of the day was Mooneyes the coon owl. Dez and I found him up in the witching room right where we'd last seen him. He was so glad to see Dez, I thought he'd hoot himself unconscious. After she fed him some soda crackers, he calmed down and perched himself on her shoulder, his eyes glowing green and bright, his raccoon tail twitching with joy.

Grandma Ester offered to try and conjure him right again, but Dez wouldn't allow it.

"He's perfect just the way he is," said Dez, scratching the top of his head. "Aren't you, fella?"

Mooneyes cozied up against her neck and flopped his long tail over the top of her head like a hat.

As we drifted off in the hot-air balloon, leaving Moaning Marsh behind for what I hoped was the very last time, Grandma Ester pointed her witching stick down at the house and called out—

"Sod swallow!"

A tremendous gurgling noise rose from the swamp below. Then the whole hilltop—house, barn, and all—sank into the black water of the marsh.

"Let's pray that does it," said Mama. "There's no telling what mischief Agnes and Serena left behind."

Grandma Ester sighed heavily. "Now that the gift is back, there'll be every sort of trouble. There's plenty of other Dredmoores who'll be happy that the curse is broken. Some of them even worse than Agnes. It won't be easy keeping the cauldron safe."

They went quiet for a while, gazing out on the dying sunset.

"I would've expected Serena to be the one chosen," said Mama after a while. "She was always so much cleverer than Agnes . . . always the one in charge."

"Don't forget," said Grandma, "it was a dark magic Choosing. Agnes must've been the most rotten of the bunch . . . the one with the blackest heart. The others must've each had some tiny speck of goodness buried under the cobwebs."

"Hard to believe," said Mama.

I thought back on Serena's phony smile and all the times she'd pretended to like me. Maybe there'd been a splinter of truth underneath it all. Despite her tricks and treachery, I couldn't help but feel sorry for her now. I looked down on the rolling forest below, hazy orange in the fading daylight, and I pictured Serena, now a black-winged raven, fluttering tree to tree, raging and restless, Agnes swooping sulkily behind her. I couldn't help but wish her well.

Later that evening, Mama came to my room to say good-night. She had a troubled look on her face, and I knew what was on her mind. My jaw went tight. She struggled to get the words out.

"I'm . . . I'm sorry I never told you, Elijah."

I sat on my bed, fiddling with a crystal radio. I didn't do her the favor of looking up.

"You had a right to know," she pushed on. "I always hoped the gift might've passed you by . . . because of your father's blood, I mean."

I shrugged. "It doesn't matter."

She moved closer and put her arm around me. "No . . . it does matter. It *does*. The gift is part of *you* . . . who you are . . . like it or not. It's *your* blood, *your* family. I had no right to keep it from you. But I was so certain the curse had put an end to it all. I thought you were safe . . . and there'd be no need to explain." She brushed the hair away from my eyes. "I didn't want you to worry."

I looked up, the truth of her words stinging my ears–*I didn't want you to worry.*

Maybe if I hadn't been so fearful of everything, she would've trusted me with the truth. She wouldn't have needed to protect me.

"I don't blame you for being mad at me." She shook her head. "There's no hiding from who we are, Elijah. It was foolish of me to think we could. Best we can do is choose how to use the gifts we've got."

I thought of Phineas Dredmoore's grave marker, and spoke the words aloud without realizing it–

"Some things you choose. Some things choose you."

Mama smiled at me, her eyes mournful and proud at the same time.

She reached inside her barn coat and pulled out a willow stick. It was kind of crooked and beat-up looking. When she held it out toward me, the tip gave off a soft silvery glow.

"I've had this hidden away for a long time," she said. "I want you to have it now. Things have changed, Eli. You've changed. You've got the Dredmoore gift in you. It chose *you.*"

I wrapped my fingers around the stick, and it glowed brighter. Then, slowly, the light faded until there was only a faint glimmer around the tip. It looked like nothing more than a trick of the moonlight.

She leaned over and kissed me on the forehead.

"Goodnight, Eli."

"Goodnight, Mama."

The Witches of Dredmoore Hollow

ᘒ᷍ᘉ

I lay awake for a long time that night, watching my witching stick shimmer on the bed stand. My trouble-bug, Jonah, snoozed peaceful as could be in his little tin house, curled up under a maple leaf. His bristly fur had turned from brown to brilliant yellow, as if my time away had done him good.

I went to the window and peered toward the graveyard. The woods lay silent and still in the pale moonlight, not so much as a breeze in the treetops. Who would've believed all the strange things that had transpired out there only a few nights before? I wondered what had become of the haunts who'd been summoned for the Choosing—my dark magic kin. Those who'd refused to let go of their earthly longings and move on to the Hereafter. It was sobering to think about all those who had come before me, Dredmoores and others. I hoped Mama would tell me about them now that I knew the truth. Each one had a story—his own choices, her own trials and fears, just like me. Some of those stories would chill my bones, no doubt; others would fill me with pride and wonder. I wanted to hear them all.

I fell asleep lying on top of the blanket, fully dressed, Jonah's tin house sitting next to me. I slept sounder than I would've expected, given all I'd been through and the unsettling prospect of what lay ahead.

The next morning, I woke with the sun falling hard on my eyes. It took me a while to get my bearings. For a moment, I wondered whether the past few weeks had all been a dream—my aunts, the cauldron, and everything that happened up on Moaning Marsh. I rolled over and buried my eyes in the pillow, as if I could postpone the day. Something tickled the back of my hand. I put my fingers to my jaw and felt something fine and wispy. It was softer than the one I'd grown under the witching maids' tonic. So soft that you could hardly call it a whisker at all.

I tucked my witching stick under the pillow and gazed out the window at the wooded hills of Dredmoore Hollow, and Clabberclaw Mountain beyond. The world was bright and beckoning. Who could guess what mysteries were out there waiting?

The sweet smell of Poppers' world-famous apple fritters wafted up the stairs into my room, calling me to breakfast.

I was more than happy to oblige.